SHOTS
IN
THE
DARK

SHOTS
IN
THE
DARK

Jack Oakley

OSEL BOOKS
San Rafael

"The Tragedy of KL" was published in *Weird Tales from Shakespeare,* edited by Katharine Kerr and Martin H. Greenberg, DAW, 1994.

"Fiat Silva" was published in *Enchanted Forests,* edited by Katharine Kerr and Martin H. Greenberg, DAW, 1995.

Book and cover design by Glenn Claycomb.

ISBN: 978-1-940121-08-6

Published by Osel Books
San Rafael, California
www.oselbooks.com

Printed in the United States of America

CONTENTS

Dog Boy

A dusty place on a hot afternoon. The dirt beneath our feet packed hard by the feet of other children running to the playfield from the mottled brown building which shades a few feet of earth behind the Oglala boy who faces me.

Beyond the field are hills brown in the heat and a few houses, two or three, low dun habitations in the brush beyond, and farther off are faraway peaks against the immense pale sky.

In the shaded dirt is a patch of mud made of spit and pee, peed upon defiantly and spat upon for good measure and mixed by the foot of the boy who then turned to me and spoke.

The familiar smell of wet dirt, of dirt and spit and acrid pee, of the soil and the people on it, people who spit on things others have built, who pee on their own playground. The hot familiar tang of incontinent earth permeates the air as the boy awaits my response. He has straight black hair in shiny bangs, black eyes big and round surrounded by dark brown skin, and he has just said something to me, something about his making of the mud, a challenge calling for a response.

I will respond but at this moment there is nothing in my mind but the moist hot smell.

Of random memories like this my life was made.

Prairie Dog Boy ran from place to place
In search of mother and father
Under the wide blue sky,
The wide blank sky.

Mother moon and father sun together shone,
But the sky was wide,
The sky was blank.

Prairie Dog Boy searched for earth mother and earth
The two who gave him rest,   father,
The two warm ones,
Ones like him, his chest, his head.

Sun father and moon mother were big and strong,
All-mother and all-father,
But the deep black sky and bland blue sky were not like
                                                           him.
Prairie Dog Boy ran from place to place
Sniffing for warmth.

We run from place to place sniffing for warmth, making
nests, sometimes wondering where we are and how we got
here. Myself, I remember where I came from and from where
to there and when and these memories locate me in space and
time so I've never been lost. New places may be unfamiliar
and even uncomfortable, but knowing how I got there gives
me a sense of self, a personal history, a foundation and base
for exploration. I am who I am because certain things happened in this or that place or I thought or felt thus and made
the choices that brought me here. I don't know what I am,
but I know how I got here.

Once I stood beside a wooden bench under a small group
of plane trees at the corner of a cobblestoned square that sloped
down and away on both sides. On other benches sat old men
wearing black hats and dark Sunday morning unshaven faces.
Several boys and a girl ran and played, shouting and quarrel-
ing and laughing. Behind me, rising above the dense narrow
Mediterranean streets through which I had come, was a field
of boulders that could well conceal a man in flight. The day
was very warm, almost hot, and hatless under the sun in a

light blue sky I was just beyond the edge of comfort.

Two old women on the bench made room for me, and for a few moments I fully reposed. It was a peaceful break from powerful walking. Where was I going? Why? I don't remember, but in new places I walk alone for hours because I want to see the place and have no one to walk with.

The people spoke another language (Spanish? Portuguese?). I could communicate little more than basic needs. Sometimes I am anxious in a strange town but here I was not. The people did not overflow with hospitality but they were amicable, responded with smiles to my greeting, continued chatting and reading the newspaper, observed me with relaxed curiosity, and let me relax as a stranger among them.

My history is also made from this memory. I am who I am in part because in my youth I charged throughout the countryside exploring and one afternoon sat peaceably among a group of strangers in a small-town square.

But I may not actually have been to that square. I have never been in Portugal. And as I piece together the itinerary of my one unaccompanied trip to Spain, I realize that I did not travel through a place like that. Was it Italy, then, or southern France? Unlikely. A scene from a movie? And the field of boulders: Now I think that I read of them and a fleeing man—or band of warriors?—in a Portuguese novel or medieval Spanish poem.

When I was young I could quickly call up the sequence of events that had brought me where I was. Now I discover that not only was I not in some places where I remember being, I sometimes no longer remember what I remember having remembered. It seems, then, that my personal history is at least partly based on what I have forgotten or merely imagine having done.

Maybe memory and imagination come to the same thing— an impression in the brain, a neural nexus that when activated recalls an earlier state of mind. When the impression is made by something that happens I call it historic, and if not, imagined. Although my sense of self—which includes what I imagine and think and feel as well as what I recall having done—is not shaken by a flaw in recollection, my history is unreliable to the extent that I can't distinguish among the sources of the impressions.

This is disturbing. In four days I will be fifty. As I continue to age, will I lose my sense of presence? Not so much who I am, because apart from a vague sense of continuity I've always felt that I am mostly defined by the situation I'm in; rather, my sense of the route I took. You could say that my identity—who I think I am—consists of knowing my history. I accept whatever happens to me and observe my reactions. My self consists of what happens to me and my reactions to it and memories of earlier reactions. If I can't remember how I got here, I'm lost. Worse: I'm no longer myself. I'm afloat.

> Behind us a story but half understood
> Barely starts to illumine this shadowy wood
> Where we find ourselves wondering whence we arrived
> And which way we should best now begin.

From a high school class only one of light's four effects on architecture remains: "Light reveals and conceals." I quickly forgot the other three and puzzled over that one for years. I remember things that stand out somehow, in this case by my lack of understanding. Further, to my detriment, once I see how things fit together I forget the details. I take notes to retrieve them later.

The act of writing helps to fix impressions, to set them in memory. And I can reaffirm or correct a recollection against the record. I have also jotted down events that I didn't understand so that one day when I had the time I could figure out what happened, or discover the habits that constitute me, the patterns in what I did, or at least learn why I remember some things and not others.

But I've been loath to wear out my memories or muddy their freshness with later, overlaid thoughts. It would be a shame to lose their purity. I suppose that understanding would be worth the sacrifice, but still I await the clarity of mind to make the risk worthwhile.

Prairie Dog Boy ran from the Great Plains and tribal mountains and basins and ranges to larger towns and the City and then to the World. Childhood in isolated western grandeur, flowering youth in the grandeur of civilization, and maturity, a job and a family in not very grand circumstances—always feeling that this progression was preparation for something and wondering what that was.

Each of us begins at zero and our long effort of fitting things into what we've learned vanishes with our death. And so we want to share what we find, add another pattern to the library, save someone else a little time. What if each had to discover everything for himself? Were it not for transmitted knowledge we would have no electricity, no screws, no central heat, no cheese. Were it not for culture we would not know-strangers. At least, not in the present profusion.

Vicarious experience is as real as that which we undergo. Were it not for the vicarious experience offered by art, we would search far and long for many lifetimes to encounter as many events.

But you, Dog Boy, have you much to teach? Others have thought more deeply about things and expressed themselves better than you ever could.

I've learned a lot of things—
How to start a Ford on a cold morning,
How to find a coon hound lost in the river downs,
How to put yourself forward without seeming;

And I've been beautiful places—
A valley falling easterly off buttes crowned with trees,
  highway following the near flank into town, somewhere
  in the West it was, Wyoming maybe, or Montana—
They begin to blend together.

I'll never no more share with you my own dear fond ones
    what I knew.
You'll never know what I took so long to learn—
Nor will I no more now anyhow—
There's more I've known than I can now recall.

Now and then you poetize about some inconsequential
situation, an instant on a hot, stinking playground, say, to
make someone feel something you felt. Why? Because others
have done the same for you. They took the trouble to write
and let you into their minds. You thank them by creating for
others this pleasure of seeing things differently. You want
to share the wonder of being here, the uncanniness of being
here at all, the surprise of sensation.

It's inane to say we make art to live on after death. When
you're gone, you're gone. Some of Shakespeare's sonnets assert
that they were written so his beloved would live on (though
as it turns out he is the one we remember), but neither his
beloved nor he live on—it is what he wrote that endures. And
note that he wrote for the living, not posterity: Those sonnets
were meant for seduction.

You, Dog Boy, are you trying to sneak some of your inconsequential past into a would-be essay on the mutability
of memory? Could you not choose more worthy memories
to inflict than the smell of piss and mud in the middle of no-
where? A series of sunsets on beaches, say, which burst and
then fade into the months and years of quotidian life, and
return when the sun sinks again on another beach?

I have driven down into towns I cannot recall, although
I begin to think my loss of recollection matters less than I
used to. These days I immerse myself in the moment, which
might exacerbate my filing memory. My sense of self is weak-
ening, too. These may be related, though my self seems to
be becoming reconstituted as simply the sum of what I feel
at a given moment.

All my life, as if with the compulsion of instinct, I've surrounded myself with random sticks I've gathered and shiny things I've made. When it comes down to it, I think we make art because we like pretty things. Now I find that nothing comes closer to something I can call me than this comforting nest I've made of thought and memory.

I would prefer to recall when I think of childhood something other than stinking mud, but if I am the sum of my memories, real or imagined, and the end of my striving is to know myself through the places I think I've been, and one of those is a defiant glare in the stink of pee and mud, then so be it.

The Body of Christ

In a deserted place are short metal structures, a foot or two high, which support plastic tubes and strips of fleshy substance. One of these machines was Jesus Christ. When it was hooked up and working, it furnished power and energy.

A historian is there and a small boy he is traveling with. He tells me and the boy that it was powered by some force, maybe faith, that is no longer around, so it cannot be made to work. It was working seven years ago.

I would like to make it work again.

The historian says that seven years ago it was already in bad disrepair but a young man arrived and made it work for a short time. He derived energy from it, and for a while there were many people here.

The aura of his former presence is strong in the area.

I say I want to make it work. The man laughs and says that was seven years ago, as if to imply that now it is impossible.

But a Voice replies to him: It was impossible until Xerxes Zinfandel came to make it run again.

I am Xerxes Zinfandel.

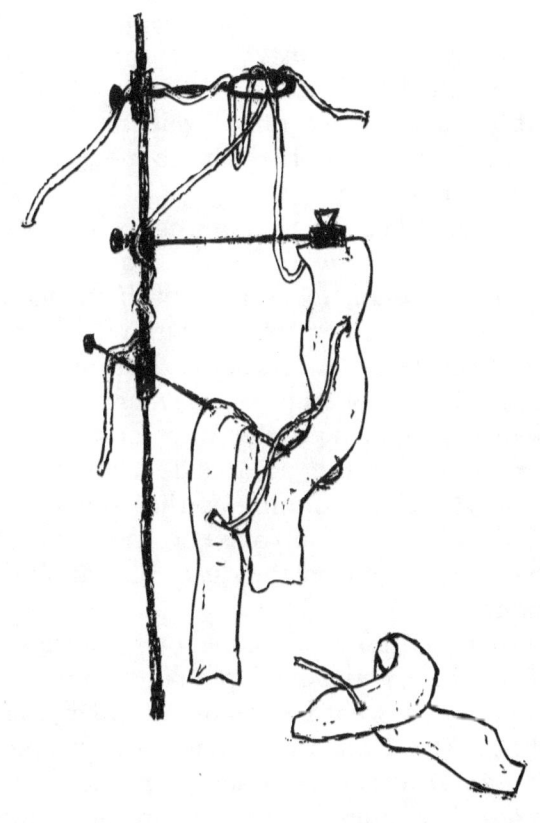

The Sun is Dragging Us by a Chain

We droned along a highway on a hot summer afternoon. My little brother was on the front seat next to me and beside him was one of my sisters, and in the back were others, maybe sisters and friends of theirs. We were on a nondescript road through one of the wide Western spaces, it was late afternoon, and the air was dusty. The sun was just above a long plateau on our left. The sisters were chattering and I was peaceably chauffeuring, only semiconscious in a highway daydream. Then my brother said to me, very matter-of-fact, merely pointing it out:

Look, Jack. The sun is dragging us by a chain.

It was a little boy who said that knowing nothing about poetry and metaphor, nor even much about chains, and surely not the literal senselessness or figurative accuracy of his utterance. That was all he said. no indication of the size of the chain, or the mass of its links, or where it was attached. Or whether we were being dragged in the direction of the sun or swung radially along an arc. It was just a comment like "There's an antelope running up that gulch." I was startled, and I listened to see if anyone else had heard. No one had. I looked at the sun over the dusty plateau and tried to see the chain.

I didn't ask him what he meant, because I thought that poetry and the experience of epiphany shouldn't be analyzed. So I don't know what he meant. I replied something like, "Yes it is, isn't it." Then his attention turned elsewhere, but part of my own attention has always rested on him, watching and praying over him, because my brother is a poet and may someday be able to hand me the key to the Door.

WINTER

The sun rises like dirty blood and the trees are so black and ugly that I'm nauseous and want to flee. The sky is topsy-turvy and horridly oppressive like an inverted Martian desert. The city rumbles awake and people carry on despite the menace. I shudder, but I'm drawn to the window. The trees are dragging us by chains. Winter has bound us in cold steel and pulls the concrete knot tighter. The cold is mad. Orion rules the glittering sky and his dog tracks the frozen waste.

SOLITUDE

A time of ambulant claustrophobia, of forced marches through the streets—if I stop moving the world will slam shut around me—I stifle if I sit still—when I slow down a nasty buzz envelops me—it's hard to hear properly—I tromp until my eyes glaze from exhaustion, matter sloshes around and spills from my eyelids—knees and ankles are jabbing darts with every step but eventually settle into a monotonous throb and I walk in a mist of pain—my skin is a rubber mannequin—but then arrive tentative alpha modulations which float my phobia beyond the streets and the rippling boundaries of my mind chime with harmonies from outside.

I ambulate in dreams of crowded stores, burning beaches, hunchbacks with disappearing deformities, phony toilets tricking the eye but not the ear—I hear everything—I am behind the illusion of substance, the delusion of action, personality and desire, hope and disgust—I send a few telepathic messages over the lines—(the post office a blazing grid in the gloom of solitude and ignorance—do they know, those dwarfs who sort the mail, that their hands glow with electrical fire?—that they sort photonic emissions from the other side of the planet?)—I play a few duets with salesgirls on the speech harmonium—I stagger down the boulevards, spittle drying at the corners of my mouth, smoke rising from my footprints, sparks in the gloaming from my arthritic elbows...

...at home staring blankly at the walls and books in an eddy of the flux I take up my guitar and transpose some of the omniplenitude into discrete fluid vibrations in this time and space—the sound picks me up and carries me—I float with it, attached to it—no longer freefalling—and return to the woody texture of the sounding box—the chair beneath me, typewriter on the desk, my reflection in the mirror, the reflection of the room—images—the room, the room repeated—I laugh and determine to install a second mirror so I can revel in repetition—a sybaritic sameness—I do a perfunctory soft-shoe at the walls—no need for more—nobody but me knows or cares if the walls are there or not—

—I'm cloistered but the phobia is gone—I know the reality of barren suffocating walls and streets but am aware of other seasons besides—I chortle—snuggle into bed and await the next phobia.

ENCIRCLEMENT

They're all sitting in a ring outside your house waiting for you to step out the door to pounce on you and beat you with clubs and then cut off small pieces of flesh. You move around inside more and more quietly, listening intently, trying to determine how many there are, where they are positioned, what they are doing. Quieter and quieter you move and then stop moving so they can't track your movements, and finally you are afraid to breathe deeply in case they hear the exhalation.

You open the door and see that there's no one there so you quickly grab a coat and walk to the sidewalk, happy that you've gotten past them this time.

But when you return, you'll have to run the gantlet.

It's okay inside where they can't get you with the windows closed and the door locked, and it's okay outside a certain distance away where you are protected by the streetlights and the number of people. The dangerous zone is the area encircling your house.

Saturday Night

This from a night in The City wherein sprout, transmogrify and die organs and tumors of thousands of shared lives:

Contact budded, bloomed and spread its mawkish scent through bleary rooms of drunkenness, faded in a hallway, and wilted in the kitchen:

Slowly engaging the gears with a couple of beers over at Steve's to sup on hamburgers and paranoid economic theories tying together the Mormons, Mafia, CIA, and a newcomer, the Vatican, which according to sources who might know now owns more than half the privately owned land in the country (and gaining daily; consider for a moment the last will and testament of one Grace Estep, formerly of Placerville, Colorado, by which is deeded some twenty thousand acres of prime grazing land to the Subsidiary Order of Carmelite Brothers, and these within carbine range of the million acres of prime grazing land on the other side of the hill which will fall into the hands of the aforementioned Mormons on the death of old Marie Scott, presently of Ridgeway; wowie! we'll have an old-fashioned jihad raging among the faithful in our own back yard! but we know we won't because the axis is firm between Rome and Salt Lake), maintains mistresses for its cardinals and a standing army in northwestern Ethiopia, and has the actual mummified body of Christ stashed away in a cellar under St Peter's:

Contact is finally made in this manner with black Stanley the actor, painter, sculptor, poet, playwright, flautist, shipbuilder nobody can tell whether he's jiving or not, but he's as paranoid as the rest of us so he's okay; also here takes place a trip down the street to invite the Guys Upstairs to my housewarming:

23

The housewarming is twice as big as the apartment; people are lined up in rows on the floor and grabbing walls for balance, anyone else would have to sit in the john talking to the shower curtain; conversation has gone from conspiracy to comparisons of modern novels—there are a couple inveterate veterans of English Lit exclaiming on the floor and bed—and everyday theater and roles and interesting jobs, which boils down how to beat the conspiracy by joining it, how to get along, and this is summed up by a request for another gin and tonic; we're all well oiled, warmed up right nice; people start bugging out to other parties, car engines turning over and catching, laughter, eyes radiating light:

For this is the exact center of the weekend
Where the week's contact was made on the sidewalk just before the group splintered; we had started together, built a common evening from shared food and talk and drink and simply the amount of time we had been together, but then on the sidewalk it passed as in twosomes and trios or singly we made off for other parts of the night, beginning now the personal business of brainkill and communal chaos, the other side of the mirror:

Then the city turned its alien side, its glyptic lights and morphic valleys and hills surrounding as we careened through the Richmond, the Haight, the Castro, into the Mission, the city percolating here sullen slogans on the walls and there up the street a lingering odor of stale orgasms that took place in another time, among other streets, only the odor seeping and seeking remembrance, forcing its presence on the present (there is a prior knowledge of the city, a déjà vu that is jamais too, making a weird overlay of past, present and possible); now here finally was a cave in the cement wallfront cliffs, a long hallway leading to the interior of the other side:
Wherein blared the deafening music that covers the spaces between people, further insulating each person, each component of confusion; the mists of noise and alcohol swirled in the

rooms and any touch was broken at its inception by a skittish
retreat to another shifting group; impossible to transcend and
anyway the etiquette of chaos demands that contact stay at
the surface; so there was only to get drunk to avoid the blunder of indecision or the blunder of uncalled-for decision like a
puppy pissing at a dinner party; a lot of people there, strangers, outgrowths of the city who knew their roles, or maybe
not, but earlier talk of roles had cast patterns on the whole
night; rebounding from group to wall the newcomer from the
country tried to figure these things out and act as expected,
and sniffed amyl nitrate and floated drunkenly around trying
to decide if there was a conspiracy or not and deciding not,
that it was merely a romantic delusion, or if there was then it
was not aimed at anybody in particular or at least at nothing
worse than undermining all chance of understanding, and we
have lived with strangers before have we not and know well
the protocol of newness which prescribes bland silence and
attention, for not until later are new characters accepted, not
until duration has established familiarity (but this only after
ugly gratuitous drunken comments on certain relationships
and particular people, which are simply ignored and soon
hopefully forgotten
    man, you are a silly boy
    talkin like a drunk
    your social life is sunk
    now everybody knows your brain is in your toes
    your ass is in a can
    boy, you are a silly man!):
    Until finally the survivors got down to it, only the hard-
core were left chatting sedated in the kitchen two hours before
dawn, but that didn't last long for it had been a long road and
exhaustion and boozed crashed down behind eyeballs and
even the hardcore scattered:
    And the city carried on with this small transfusion and
many small others coursing through its concrete arteries feeding the great organism, the creature that lives through the
lives of its inhabitants, groans and feels chaotic life.

San Francisco 1974

They say a third of the men are gay and another third alcoholic. To which I would add that a third of the women are in the movement and another third twisted by the civil service. Then there are the winos, the freaks, the foreigners, the tourists and everybody else who doesn't live here, the one or two artists and the thousands of pseudo artists. Everybody here has a trip, which is okay, but they are all trying to Lay It Down on everybody else.

But for all that or maybe because of it there is tolerance for everything and everyone. The city is absolute potentiality, a place of freedom where you can rise to your own level, do and be what you want without outraging or shocking other inhabitants. Since I feel no pressure to be anything I'm becoming myself, finding my natural impulses and letting them run without inhibition.

But how do I meet a normal person? Would any normal person move to this city? If everybody who lives here is weird, what does that make me? And what right do I have to complain about anyone else?

SUMMER

87 in the shade and flies batted themselves against windowpanes. 95 on the sidewalk. The sun was up there in the sky and on Kearney Street they were dropping like faded daisies and the clocks flashed what seemed to be the temperature—10:04, 11:00, just drop a zero—streetlights wilted in the glare and old ladies in black veils stumbled swooning into lobbies crying, "Where's the fog? This is summertime!"

The streets were piled with litter and orange peels, awaiting next winter's rain to wash them.

Anthropomorphic claptrap. It was I who awaited next winter's cleansing rain. The streets did nothing but be vehemently there.

Next fall I would start at State in engineering. I had bought a pocket calculator that was good for nothing but checking the phone bill, so I had to make it useful. No, really, I wanted to learn engineering so I knew what Max was talking about. Actually it was because my great-uncle was an engineer for the Acheson, Topeka & Santa Fe, though it turned out he didn't drive trains. He was an electrical engineer.

Well, well, it would be a long row to how I mean hoe.

i & joe & max

the resolution

we're all losers around here, me & my friends, here on the alley. it's like joe was saying last night, we're all over the hump or past the peak, i don't know just what he was saying because i wasn't listening all that close, there wasn't any point in it & he was losing the argument anyway.

but it got me thinking, about the hump or peak or what-ever it is. i've already passed the peaks i was looking forward to. mathematics at fourteen & virility at nineteen & craps at twenty. peaked on jesus at eleven and pike's at twenty-two. i remember in p.e. they said girls grow faster than boys through their teens but the boys catch up around eighteen, well that's one peak i haven't reached yet maybe but it's six years later so i guess i won't count too hard on it.

i'm five foot two & joe he's six two so he peaked on that one all right but he only weighs one ten so i guess he lost something else somewhere along the line. one thing though is he's so long he can hide that foot & a half dagger he carries down his pant leg & nobody ever notices or if they do they think it's his privates which is as skinny as the rest of him.

& a good thing too because last night this clown pulls my .32 out of my armpit, you know i tell you i wondered what he was doing in there, & shoots out the schlitz advertisement by the cash register & the hell of it was, was he didn't pull it very far out before he fired it & now i'm deaf in that ear ex-cept for a bad ringing.

& me almost deaf anyway from the bomb they threw in

28

max's car last month.

i was plenty pissed off about it & of course it got real quiet in there right away & then was my chance to say something about it but joe didn't give me a chance. he had his privates out & under that monkey's shoulder blade before i could say anything, but i probably couldn't have thought of anything to say anyway.

& then what, i don't know except it's my left ear & after we left joe walked on that side & i had to keep asking him to repeat what he said until we changed sides.

joe was laughing about it, he has a huge gut splitting grin & he thought it was funny, because max had just gotten me a job as a listener, like a coffee taster except it's for recordings of crickets, that was going to be the first job i'd had since pinkertons went broke, & everybody was saying now i'd have a steady job & income & pretty soon i'd move up to cicadas & eventually locusts & one of these days i'd move off the alley to some snazzy joint, & now here i was deaf & probably out of a job & there was joe splitting his gut about it.

well, it was funny & i laughed too but i swore i'd get even & that sobered joe up right away. he can't stand swearing.

"look andy" he said "stabbing a guy in the back in a bar fight is one thing but getting even with the whole crowd isn't the same thing. & budweiser is brewing up a big one this time. didn't you see those anti-skid riot shoes that joker had on? your everyday drunk doesn't walk around in shoes like that."

"yah joe" i said "but i'm getting sick & tired of sitting around & letting this stuff happen, you know i'm sick & tired of it & what about my goddamn ear anyway."

ii
joe becomes disposed

"look andy" joe said "why don't we go waste some of those skid street bums instead, work off some nervous energy, you're all worked up about this. look at me i'm cool as a cuke & after all it's me has to go face up to the seagram 7 about this honky. i mean it was your .32 & all but it was my privates got stuck in him & look at me am i upset, no i am like i said cuke."

"yah well ok" i said "ok it was you did it but it's nothing permanent because you know & i know the 7 is leaning toward schlitz these days & you'll be out of there with nothing worse than a six volt electro-shock if that & you know it but me i am now deaf you know i wanted that job & now i have lost it, goddamn, i am going to get even."

"andy i wish you wouldn't swear so much" said joe & he real quick jerked my arm & pulled me away from getting run over by some gook in a ferrari with budweiser plates.

i screamed and tried to crawl up joe's shoulders to get some distance between me & danger.

"andy" said joe "you are very nervous tonight" & he gently set me down on the sidewalk. there was a sound like a snarling cat & then one like an empty beer bottle hitting the pavement after falling three stories except it was my head it was hitting & i fell over. when i opened my eyes & looked around everything was blurry, the lights were blurry & so was joe's face bending over me.

"bottle launchers" he was saying "somebody's using bottle launchers."

"joe" i moaned "now i'm losing my eyesight, how old are you supposed to be for your best eyesight. i'm over the hump joe i tell you all of a sudden my eyes aren't working like they were."

"andy" said joe solemnly "andy you're losing things too fast & i just thought of something, the thought just came to me that everybody we know is a loser, even max is a loser in his own way but you are a bigger loser even than the rest of us, you are losing much too fast to be normal, in fact andy, i might even say somebody is out to get you, nobody loses as much as fast as you do."

"i can hardly hear you joe, talk in my other ear."

"in fact andy, i think i know who is out to get you but why & why you, well why not after all i suppose. how are your eyes?"

i said they were better because they were, a little. joe is a nice guy. he helped me up & brushed me off & took my arm & we walked along.

"it's the beer companies andy, i've suspected them for a while now & that bottle launcher seals it. do you realize this is big andy big & not only that it's international, that bottle that hit you was a dos xx."

"yah i guessed as much" i said "only the mexicans have such lousy bottle launchers they sound like squalling cats."

"well andy you know you owe me your life for that ferrari & even though it doesn't matter who owes who what of course because if it did we wouldn't have time for anything else, i am still an honorable man & wish to settle this debt before it becomes a problem so i feel i owe it to you to help you get even & i will."

"joe" i said "no really you don't have to, this is my business & as for saving my life, forget it."

"andy i cannot, i insist, i owe it to you."

"come on joe i hate talking about things like this" i began but he cut me off.

"goddamn it andy we're going to get even with those bastards, on my great aunt's virgin maidenhead."

"joe!" i cried "you swore!"

"i know i know" he muttered "let's go get max."

iii
i & joe kill some time

so we walked up to the y on grease street where we knew max would be swimming because that's what he does that time of night. we walked & sat down on the sofa in front of the window they have so you can watch the swimmers & waited so we could catch max's eye but he was wearing goggles to keep the water out & didn't see us.

"geez they look funny" i said "just swimming back & forth & back & forth & now & then they stop & rest & then they just start swimming back & forth again."

"yah they do" said joe "but if you want to be a good

swimmer you gotta do it that way, i used to be a good swimmer so i know."

"sure" i said "& what's the peak age for a swimmer."

"fifteen" said joe & then he was quiet.

i could see i'd made him feel bad so to get his mind off it i said "hey joe how's your woman these days."

"oh i saw her today" he said "walking in as she naked came from the bathroom & he naked bashfully hid in the closet, then offered me a shot of whiskey which it was not, it was bourbon, & he calls himself a poet."

"oh joe" i said.

"& then she said i'm sorry i can't talk but i'm busy now & i have to take a bath & then cook breakfast & then clean my room & go for a walk, & i said fine give me a call now & then so i know what's up & she said ok & if you move let me know your address & i said what? but you know this already & as if i was going to move anyway."

"oh joe" i said.

"so i picked up the hammock she brought back for me & said goodbye & left with a clear heart & a conscious head & all debts settled, though like i say about debts anyway."

"oh joe" i said "i'm sorry i brought it up."

"it's ok" said joe "it doesn't matter. but you would think a poet would know the difference between bourbon & whiskey wouldn't you."

max came up & said "hi you guys listen andy a terrible thing happened about that cricket job, they already hired somebody with experience in cockroaches & piss me off, they told me you could have it but now there's nothing i can do about it shit i'm sorry."

"that's ok max" i said "i'm deaf now anyway."

iv
max is convinced

"listen max" said joe "they're trying to get andy here & things are getting serious, we have to do something."

"oh yah?" said max & he looked at me sideways "what would they want to pick on poor little andy for, you sure you guys aren't just imagining things."

"no" said joe "why just now they were taking pot shots at him with a greaser bottle launcher & before that they tried to run him down & before that when we were over at charlie's there was some funny business about a schlitz advertisement, you know the one that lights up by the cash register or used to."

"used to huh" said max, not being slow to pick up on things like that.

"yah" i said "we'll tell you all about it but right now let's get out of here before they try to drown us in that pool."

we walked out on the street to where max parked his motorcycle. he has a sidecar so all three of us can go places but we couldn't go anywhere right then because there was a car parked in front of it blocking it.

"nuts" said max "& i put this big sign on the windshield saying please no parking & it's a no parking zone anyway, people have no consideration."

he took a ballpeen hammer out of the toolbox & smashed the driver's side window & unlocked the door & got in & rolled it out of the way.

"max" joe exclaimed.

"i know just how you feel" i said.

"let's get out of here" said max & he handed around goggles & hopped on & joe hopped on behind him & i crawled in the sidecar & we took off.

i asked where we were going but what with the noise from the motorcycle & being deaf i couldn't hear what they said so i settled back & shut my eyes. i could still see enough to be scared by the way max drives.

all at once the noise diminished & i opened my eyes & saw joe & max up ahead of me & i was alone coasting slower & slower in the middle of the bay bridge & traffic was screeching around trying to miss the sidecar so i closed my eyes again & then somebody didn't miss.

when i started feeling again i couldn't feel my legs but i

could hear max saying to joe "but how did they know he was going to be in the sidecar."

"i don't know" said joe "but as you see they did."

"you guys" i said "i can't feel my legs now, this has got to stop."

"what did you say" said joe "we can hardly hear you."

"i can't feel my legs" i shouted.

"ok ok we can hear you."

"thank god" i said "i thought i was losing my voice too, this has got to stop."

"you're right" said max "nobody can fall apart as fast as you are andy, did you realize that."

"yes" i said.

"do you realize what this means andy."

"yes max" i said.

"somebody is out to get you andy."

"thank you max" i said.

"sheesh does he have to be sarcastic" said max.

"well" said joe "he's the one that's falling apart."

letters to max

dear max, it seems we was sittin in the park yesterday afternoon listening to the music of eire when a ditty tripped out of the bandshell & landed in poor joey's lap & ever since he's been a little frontheavy but it's ok, he's overweighted behind & anyway he says now when his stomach rumbles people think it's st patrick's day & they do a little jig & say things like bloody british & begorrah & joey gets a kick out of that & says he wouldn't give it up for all the geese in the fen.

dear max, it seems we was up at coit tower yesterday lookin at the bay when summer crept in through the golden gate on catty little feet & didn't stop til it climbed up poor joey's shoulder, his left one, & ever since he's been sorta weighted down on that side but it's ok because he's righthanded & anyway he says there's nothing like a cool summer fog to carry around & relax in when the sun gets too hot which everybody says it has been lately so they're all glad when they see joey comin along.

dear max, it seems we was walkin through chinatown yesterday lookin for some taiwan firecrackers when the new year dragon slithered up & clamped onta poor joey's thigh, his left one, & ever since he's been sorta weighted down on that side but it's ok, he useta limp on his other side & anyway the dragon has ruby eyes so the chinese all say to each other, look how lucky that guy is he has a ruby dragon & some of the kids even run up to pet it & they laugh a lot & joey likes kids so he likes that.

dear max, it seems we was walkin down bush street yesterday night lookin for a nipponese restau whereat to fill our bellies when springtime leapt over the transamerica pyramid & latched onta poor joey's bicep, his right one, & ever since he's been sorta weighted down on that side but it's ok, he's lefthanded & anyway he likes the attention he gets from people who say to each other, hey look at that guy he's got springtime hangin off his bicep, & some of them even run up & take a deep whiff & walk off smiling with daisies in their eyes.

dear max, it seems we was walkin up mission yesterday lookin for a swimming pool whereat to wet our backs when nightfall landed with a thud on poor joey's collarbone, his left one, & ever since he's been sorta weighted down on that side but it's ok, he's righthanded & anyway he likes it because lots of people come up & think it's nighttime & lean on his shoulder & fall asleep & then he picks their pockets but he says it's ok just think of him as a hotel for a night & that's his bill.

dear max, it seems we was walkin along the beach yesterday lookin for ships out at sea when a big earthquake jumped out of the ground & took hold of poor joey's arm, his right one, & ever since he's been sorta weighted down on that side but it's ok, he's lefthanded & anyway he's happy that people are relieved when they see it & say thank goodness there's the big earthquake, at least it won't make California slide in the ocean now & joey's glad but he says you never know where it'll go next.

how you look at it

how old am i? i asked myself. AS OLD AS THE MOUN-
TAINS, myself replied in an immense voice. no not that, i
said, i mean the other. oh, it said, twenty-five, i mean -four,
and so what? oh nothing, i said, i was just wondering.

several years later i asked again. AS YOUNG AS THE
SPRINGTIME, it answered. no no, the other, i said. oh, it
said, sixty-four, i mean -five.

myself gets confused from time to time.

one last thought, max

"'now take paradise. why fuck up paradise?' i said to them," this guy said incredulously to me. "'you got everything. you don't need nothing!'"

i would have asked "that's the finger on the problem, isn't it? how could they know? they obviously thought they needed something, so in their minds they weren't in paradise. let's say you actually are in paradise—how can you tell? it's easy to say someone else should know better, and it's easy to look back and say you should have known better yourself. what's hard is knowing when you've got it good, given that life is striving and things always change. i'd say you never do think you've got everything and need nothing."

but i had to leave for an appointment and so i deferred the pleasure of a discussion.

PLANKS

A plank extends from a third-story window, counterbalanced by a chest of drawers, and from the window across the alley another plank, ballasted by a bed and stack of chairs. Inching onto the plank from the other window is a fair-haired young woman carrying a brown paper sack containing nails and yerba mate. She reaches one-third of the distance from her window and stops. Her broadbrimmed pink hat is blown gently off her head and wafts down to the street at the corner.

Starved for Love

He knew a girl who would fall in love with him and he would fall in love with her. Her name was Candy and she was dandy.

It was a good idea, he thought, for one reason and another.

One was that he was having a hard time getting food stamps and maybe she would give him some food. He was always hungry, and he was always tired, because he stayed up late and walked around all day looking at things. When they were in love he might be able to rest now and then, and sleep peacefully at night.

That's what he thought now. When they were in love everything would be real again but he would be even more tired.

Last night he had realized he was free. The process of escaping his past and his culture, which had begun a few years ago in a fervor of adolescence, was over. He was back among men, he told his friend Joe.

"Welcome back to the everyday humdrum," Joe said. Joe was a fine one to talk, though, because he was in love himself, and talked about it a lot trying to figure out what to do.

"Don't worry," he said. "Be happy." He also told Joe he couldn't tell him anything he didn't already know and couldn't say anything that hadn't already been said. Then he said, "I don't want to get involved," but laughed to let Joe know he didn't really mean it.

"I know who you can get involved with," Joe said.

"Who?"

"Candy."

"Yeah," he said and leaned back in the chair to look out the window. "You know, I thought I was sensing something like that but wasn't sure."

Then he realized Joe had been talking about Candy. "Oh, you said Candy!"

"Yes," said Joe.

"I thought you were talking about Carrie. Yeah, Candy, I know. I picked up on that."

Joe had known her for a long time. "She's a real sharp chick," he said. "She's really intelligent, a real doll."

"Well, she's playing the fluffy female right now."

Joe didn't say anything. He didn't want Joe to think he was belittling his judgment, so he joked, "I've always been a sucker for that." Though it wasn't really a joke; he always had been a sucker for that.

They both laughed. Then they talked some more and then it was midnight and they had to get some sleep.

The next morning he went again to the food stamp place and thought about how Candy could cook up some meals with his free food, which was just as good as your typical middle class food since it was actually the same, only purchased with different money.

He got a table for the room where he was staying (a bedroom off the living room which gave onto the bathroom, another bedroom and the kitchen, which gave onto another bedroom) where he could put his typewriter.

I think I might be starving to death, so I want to write a story first, he wrote. I woke at five this morning and knew I wouldn't be able to go back to sleep for a while.

The quickest way of communicating is fucking. Statement and response are immediate. But you can't say anything very complicated that way. "My, my, how slippery and tight you are," I say and she replies, "How well you slip and slide and how big you are."

But he wanted to say something about how children are pristine and grown up people got lost somewhere outside the garden with the fountain. He wanted to point out that all structures contain in themselves the means of their own destruction, and that destruction contains the birth and the form of a new structure, and that it all comes the same thing, which is simply a bunch of children trying to build a castle on the beach for their friends to play in.

Those were the things he always tried to say afterwards, when he shouldn't say anything, when he should lie beside her and say how nice you smell, what kind of perfume do you like, take this golden necklace and wear it so you will be even more beautiful, your breasts rise like freshly baked bread and your nipples make me forget about pay stubs.

The next morning he went into the kitchen not fully awake. Lately it had been hard to tell when he was awake. There were moments when he was aware of various things, but that was all. His criteria for knowing if he was awake included being able to feel something another person was feeling. That was hard because he wasn't sure if other people felt much.

One of the girls he lived with, that is, one of the two who had sublet a room to him, always had her television on or the radio or a record. She talked in a loud voice to her dog. She worried so much about the dog that she had no time to think of people. Her world included the noises on the airwaves, the dog, and her parents, from whom she was trying to separate. She had long arguments with them on the telephone.

When he got up at five and went to the kitchen her radio was on. He wondered if she slept with it on. Whenever she was home it was on. She would burst in through the kitchen door, head for her bedroom, turn on the radio and close the door.

Once in a while she would come out of her room to tell him more rules he would have to follow while he lived there. Her name was Nancy.

The other girl was named Peggy. Peggy had a boyfriend who stayed with her a lot and they seldom ate in the house. They went out to dinner. They had many friends who telephoned or visited. Peggy spent much of her time arranging to meet friends somewhere. The rest of the time she studied. This was her last year of college.

Practically the only times Nancy or Peggy spoke to him was to let him know how they did things around the house.

Once Nancy said, "Do you know about the dishes?"

He had come in five minutes earlier and was eating eggs and tuna he'd fried together. He had seen the dirty dishes and was going to wash them when he finished eating. He hadn't eaten anything yet that day.

"No," he said.

"It's your turn to do the dishes," she said. "We take turns around here."

He had done the dishes once since he moved in, and he'd been watching and seen them be done twice since then, so he already knew it was his turn.

How can I talk to this girl? he said to himself. Anything I say she will think I am only making an excuse. It's hardly worthwhile saying anything because she is not calm enough to listen and understand.

"Each person washes the dishes in order," she said. "Although I'm not sure how well that's working out. I think we're going to have to change things. I think each person should wash his own dishes. You don't have to wash Peggy and Jim's dishes if they eat supper here. And I don't want to have to, uh…"

He completed the sentence in his head …wash your dishes, she was going to say but hesitated lest he take it wrong. The poor girl is terrified of other people, he thought, but I can't do anything about it. She'll have to learn by herself to finish her thoughts and find that I don't take offense.

"You know," she continued, "it would be better if everyone just washed their dishes after they used them."

"I think so," he said.

"Peggy and I are going shopping tomorrow," she said. She went into her bedroom and called, "Do you want to give us some money?"

"How much do you want?" He didn't think much of money. It was there to be used, you had it or you didn't, but you shouldn't treat it as though it was something different from other things. Most people did, though. They hedged around when it came to matters of money, hemmed and hawed. He preferred outright greed and clear talk.

A difference between the aristocracy and the middle class, he thought, is that the aristocracy is more plainspoken. Though not necessarily noble. Anyone could be noble but few were. They didn't even see that they could be.

Nancy hemmed and hawed.

He didn't know what to think though he knew that sooner or later he would have to give some money for food. The thing he didn't like was that because she hadn't said how much she wanted, she would have to say it another time, and when she did she would probably be upset that she had to be so explicit, and she would be angry because she had lacked the courage to ask earlier.

While he was doing the dishes she rushed in and out of the kitchen to and from the bathroom. Sounds of water running in the sink, toilet flushing, tooth brushing. She began humming when she entered the kitchen and stopped when she exited.

She closed the door to her room again. Sounds of a chair sliding across the floor, radio, underarm spray deodorant. The hiss summed her up pretty well.

She came into the kitchen with her coat and her dog. "When do you go to work?"

"Oh," he said slowly, "about a quarter to seven." He could tell she was going to ask a favor.

"Well, I'm going to put Colombo out and I wondered if you could maybe please let him back in a half hour or so." She always talked so fast and nervously that he felt constrained to talk calmly and slow.

"Sure," he said. He didn't turn from the sink because he didn't want to see her vibrate.

"I'll write a note so you won't forget."

He was amazed. Was that the sort of thing she herself forgot? Of did she have so little faith in people—in him—that she had to extend her admonishing presence?

He didn't say anything. She wrote a note, said goodbye and rushed out the door.

She was back in a second. He wasn't surprised. She dashed through the kitchen to her room and hurried back saying nothing this time.

He sighed and wondered if she would ever calm down.

Peggy didn't like it that he didn't have much money for food. "I supported a girl once who just wouldn't pay her share. I don't want to do it again. I'm sure you can understand my point of view."

"Yes," he said, because he knew what it was like to have a roommate who wouldn't pay his share.

He had tried a moment earlier to express his embarrassment about not having much money. These girls always had enough for what they needed, and what they needed was far beyond mere food and rent.

None of the people they knew didn't have enough money.

When they said, "I don't know how I'll find enough money for the rent," or, "I'm always broke. We'll have to stop eating out so much," they thought they were poor. They didn't know any poor people.

He told Peggy he would give her all the money she wanted to buy food, and that he would find enough, borrow it somewhere if he had to, to pay the rent.

She was satisfied, because the rent didn't affect her personally. That was between him and landlady Nancy. As long as he maintained his fiscal responsibilities to Peggy, they would get along fine.

"You don't like Pepsi, I see," she said. "You never drink any of it."

"No," he said. "I like it, but it's yours, so I haven't been drinking it."

"Oh! It's for everybody. I give it away. All my friends drink it. I give it to them whenever they come."

He thought she was trying to show that she was not stingy. She just didn't want him to freeload off her and Nancy.

Well, if that's the way it was, that's the way it was. He wondered why people were so stingy with their food.

When he had lived in one of four rooms on a second story and shared the kitchen with the other lodgers, whom he never saw, he put a sign on his shelf that said Please Don't Eat The Food because someone had been eating his cookies. If someone is starving, let him take some of my food, he thought, but something nourishing for god's sake, like soup, or cheese or meat, expensive as they are. But cookies? That is a luxury. If you can't afford it, leave it alone.

That's why he didn't drink Peggy's Pepsi even when she invited him to help himself. Pepsi was a frill. If she wanted to be generous, she would invite him to drink her milk. But milk was food, and the barrier applied to food, not luxuries. Affluent people share luxuries but not basics. Maybe in order to feel less guilty about things they know they don't need.

He sat in a café with his stomach churning around a large meatball sandwich and a scoop of potato salad. It felt like there was room for more, but he had no more money and anyway wasn't sure he could actually get more down. The food made him feel a little queasy.

He sat quietly and digested, not moving until the process was well begun. He didn't want to lose any nutrition to sudden movements or upset stomach or, worse, vomiting.

Before he ate, he had wondered if food would affect his state of mind. He had felt like he was floating. It was hard to concentrate on anything, hard to lose himself in reading, and impossible to summon the clarity of purpose for writing. Now he took out a pen and began to write on the back of his placemat, though it was an effort. He smoked a cigarette and slowly drank a cup of coffee. He wanted to write about the girl he had been with the night before.

She was attractive, and kind, and not the type to have intercourse on the third date. She told him she had to be in love with someone before she could make love. It had been hard not to press on, though, since they had been lying entwined on his bed and he'd had an erection most of the time.

His stomach had kept making noises. She had given him a ham and cheese sandwich and glass of milk earlier in the evening. Then they went to a bar and he spent two dollars on drinks and fifty cents for a pack of cigarettes. The cigarettes gave him a sore throat and made his nose stuffy.

He couldn't afford any of it. He should be spending his money on food.

She asked if he would date a girl if she wouldn't sleep with him. He said yes, because he wanted to know her better and figured he could find sex with others.

Two girls had hustled him earlier at the bar where he worked. They invited him to a party and one of them put her arm around him and pressed against him. She told him he was good-looking. He told her she was good-looking too, and put his arm around her. He told her he would go to the party but instead met the girl he already had a date with.

He didn't get any sex, but he was making friends with a very pretty girl. Both drives were powerful, friendship and sex.

He decided the food had improved his outlook. He felt much better, good enough to go home and write on his type-writer. He wanted to write about kindness and gentleness, to show for once the humanity of a person, instead of something edgy and clever. He paid and left.

A couple he knew invited him to dinner on Tuesdays and he hoped to have others invite him on Wednesdays and Thursdays. He spent Sundays with his family and ate so much he was sick.

He wanted to describe people, including himself, fully and honestly in their complex humanity, but to dig beneath the surface and show how it is shaped by the depths is hard work and he was too tired. Actually, it wasn't that. He was too lazy.

He thought of Candy who bebopped like a bopper, got onto the dance floor and boogied like a boogyman. She was a lot of fun and never serious. She must be serious sometimes but he wouldn't notice because he was so goddammed serious himself that anyone else would have to be catatonic before he would think they weren't being frivolous. However, she had a nice body, a very nice body.

He told himself he wouldn't fuck any chick he wouldn't want to live with, but whenever he got close to Candy his cock rose. When he kissed her and she hung back he felt a tremendous restlessness. He thought that the only place things could end was bed. He also thought that was the only place things could begin; bed was the only place for them.

If they could only live in fuck together, joined until the end of time, and she came and came and he too and it never stopped. But there would be the moment when he softened and slid out. He would roll off with nothing left but a cigarette and it would be so late at night that they wouldn't want to smoke.

If he was honest, he would show her this little essay before things went further so she knew him better and he could learn from her reaction if she had or had not some of the qualities he wanted in a girl he would live with. But he couldn't help remembering in his cock and the ache in his loins what it was like to lie in fuck, and that overrode his inclination to honesty. Then he imagined telling her nothing, revealing none of his honest thoughts and feelings but showing an attractive surface that would seduce her into bed but at the same time, in case it turned out to be only a sexual relationship that he got bored with, give enough glimpses so she would already have known by the time they broke up that they had to break up.

But nothing came of it and he never knew her body nor if she was as smart as Joe claimed.

A Piano Concert in Siberia

In a small Siberian city the audience assembled as Natasha sat on the stage at the piano vaunted by the mayor on the ride from the airport and over dinner as the only piano within five hundred kilometers, purchased and transported at great trouble only one month ago, indeed a jewel to be cherished, followed by unremitting pompous declamation during the few minutes she could have tried its touch before the performance; she sat, therefore, fully concentrated on the piece to be played, struck the first magnificent chord but produced no sound at all, nothing, started bolt upright in amazement and tried again with the same baffling result, and stood and looked into the instrument's interior with incredulous comprehension and turned to the audience to announce: "There are no strings!"

Three O'Clock

The waitress is fifty and unhurried. She has been asking everyone who comes in if it is nice outside. They all say yes. She says, "At 3:00 I am off and I'll get to go outside." She is an old woman.

At 3:00 she picks up her coat.

I say, "Enjoy yourself."

She says, "I will. Thank you." Then she says, "Enjoy yourself."

I say, "Thank you, I will."

She has her coat on and leaves to enjoy the beautiful afternoon and breathe the clear air, see the autumn leaves and feel herself walk down the sidewalk breathing the air.

Shopping Day

My sister's husband's sister told her that her cousin Eileen and Eileen's friend Sharon had been downtown shopping one afternoon. Eileen was driving the station wagon home, gabbing with Sharon and not paying any more attention to the street than she had to, when a cat ran in front of the car too fast to do anything about. She slammed on the brakes about the same time they felt a thud on the bottom of the car. Sharon shrieked.

"Shut up, Sharon," said Eileen as the car skidded and swerved. She stopped.

"Did we hit the cat?" asked Sharon.

"Oh, hell. Yes."

"Um, do you think we ought to just, um, keep on going?"

The thought was tempting. But Eileen said, "Oh, hell. No, we can't do that. Let's get out and see how bad it's hurt."

The cat lay motionless on the pavement. There was no blood. "Thank God," muttered Eileen, who had been feeling a little queasy since the thud. She peered at the cat and poked it with the toe of her shoe.

"Is it dead?"

"I think so." She prodded it again and bent down and felt it with her hand. "Oh, yeah, it's dead. I think."

"What are we going to do now, Eileen?"

"Well, I suppose we ought to find out who it belongs to."

"Are you kidding? We'll never find them. What are we going to do, walk around and knock on all the doors?"

"Well, okay, let's try a few anyway. We can't leave a dead cat in the street like this." She picked the cat up by its tail. It weighed more than she would have thought.

No one answered the first door. They rang at a second and while they waited Eileen told Sharon that if nobody came to the door here either, she was ready to quit. But a woman came and told them it looked like Mrs. Weber's cat, across the street.

Mrs. Weber said, yes, it was her cat.

Eileen told her how sorry they were, and they'd like to make amends somehow, by getting her a new cat maybe.

But Mrs. Weber didn't really care about the cat. She said she never liked the nasty thing but the trouble was, her kids did. Would Eileen and Sharon do her a favor and just take it away with them so that when the kids got home from school they wouldn't know, and then when the cat didn't come home for a few days they could assume that it had run away or something.

Relieved, Eileen and Sharon returned to the station wagon and discussed what to do with the corpse. Sharon suggested emptying one of the bags in the back and putting the cat into it for the time being, so they didn't just have a dead cat in the back. They put it in a Macy's bag and drove off.

"I could use a cup of coffee," said Sharon. "Let's stop at the mall."

"Good idea. I feel like a nervous wreck."

They parked in the vast shopping center lot. Before they went in for coffee, Eileen thought they should probably cover the bags in the back with a blanket so any thieves walking around wouldn't see anything worth taking. They put the Macy's bag on the roof while they did that. Then they headed for Eppie's Coffee Shoppe, forgetting about the bag.

They found a table by the window looking onto the parking lot and ordered coffee and coconut cream pie.

"Now what are we going to do with that cat?" wondered Eileen.

Sharon told her to take a look at a woman dressed in ratty old clothes who was wandering through the parking lot. The woman walked to Eileen's car, stopped, peered around, and then reached up and took the Macy's bag. Sharon giggled.

The woman came their way and entered Eppie's. She sat

at a table not far away and put the bag on the floor until the waitress took her order.

Finally the woman bent over and opened the bag. She sat bolt upright, turned pale, and threw up. Then she slumped sideways and slid slowly to the floor. Eileen and Sharon were speechless.

The waitress, who saw the woman collapse, ran to the manager. The manager walked hastily to the woman's table and grimaced when he saw the vomit, then crouched beside her and poked her arm. Then he told the waitress to call an ambulance and straightened out the woman on the floor. Other patrons craned their necks to see what was happening.

When the ambulance attendants entered, the woman was still motionless. They raised her with some difficulty onto a gurney and headed for the door. The manager noticed the Macy's bag. He ran with it after the gurney and balanced it carefully on the woman's stomach. The two attendants loaded the woman and the bag into the ambulance and drove away.

DATE: 7 June 72
TO: Lemming
LOCATION: Seward, Nebraska
SUBJECT: Filthy Pix
FROM: Central Committee

AA

Have received reports of recent upsurge in absurd and untasteful photographic activities. At least two instances presumed originating your locale. Description of pix follows.

BB

Half of presumed cub scout den bearing shoulder patches indicating Seward origin. Blurbs beside several scouts' heads indicate they are saying vulgar things. Suggest you trace this den and investigate "scouts." May be onto drug ring, cannibalism, queers, weapons smugglers, enemy intelligence group, underground news ring, defecatory terrorism. This on assumption that a concerned citizen is tipping us off. Suggest you also try to identify citizen, who may actually be mad antisocial loony.

CC

Snapshot taken from car window of front steps of "The Robert Frost Retirement Center" (sic). Proceed on assumption this entirely faked, as no one in right mind would be party to such a travesty of good taste. Retired citizens also have a right to dignity.

DD

Though the two pix are dissimilar, their origination in the same locale leads to suspicion of single source, confirmed by handwritten addresses. Our handwriting expert says the specimens are of an uncommon variety, the author probably subsisting on a diet of corn and sorghum, corn predominating, and given to a flip attitude.

EE

Weasel attaches great importance to this issue. He took the "Robert Frost" business as a personal insult and is preparing a punishment involving recordings of Rod McKuen. He has therefore petitioned the committee for permission to deal with the originator himself, but the committee feels graver issues are at stake. The dignity of scouting, indeed of our boys themselves, is in question. But check possibility that this den is front for something bad. Coyote wants the kid with the big smile to eat her out, but your orders are to concentrate on the asshole who sent these pix.

FF

Paragraph EE is only to keep you up to date on what's going on here. As you can see, Lemming, this business has caused an uproar.

GG

Your orders, should you accept, are to identify and take into custody the perpetrator of these vulgarities. Convey said person or persons before the committee. Expenses will be paid in the usual manner. Coyote says she's looking forward to it.

HH

Should you not accept, don't show your ugly mug around here ever again.

II

As a personal favor, Rabbit requests you also bring the mother of the kid with the smile. The committee has okayed his request.

JJ

Re Vietnamese orphan girls: Sorry, Lemming, we were unable to fulfill your request. No twelve-year-olds left.

KK

Re murder in billiard room: The committee concurs with your appraisal and directs you to punish the maid. Suggest rubber, no Vaseline, three orifice.

LL

Heh heh you lucky Lemming.

MM

Good luck and God bless.

Prairiedog
for the Central Committee

DATE: 4 October 72
TO: Central Committee
LOCATION: Placerville, Colorado
SUBJECT: Pthirus pubis
FROM: Agent L

May I leave aside form for a moment, dear brothers, and be permitted to express myself concerning those pernicious little vermin that I picked up in your fair burg? In my capacity as your agent I am of course in no wise offended by their blood-sucking little snouts, but allow me to express my disgust at the thought of having passed them on to a dear lady friend encountered in the performance of my duties, which duties consist in just this encounter of lady friends.

In fact, the incident has caused me to question my commitment to the task which you assigned to me. If in the very performance of my duties I render the subject unsuitable for future investigation, am I not defeating the purpose of my assignment? The terms of my commission were to investigate as *much* as possible, not as *many* as possible, although neither excludes the other. But my cause for doubt springs from the fact that you planted on me the eggs containing the destruction of my mission at the same time you revealed its nature. My brothers, can I trust you after such a betrayal? Or perhaps a deeper explanation escapes my poor brain?

I beg you to consider at your next convocation your solitary foreign agent afflicted on all sides by ladies and lice. He is

57

acting under your orders, after all.

Or send help!

Good luck and God bless.

APOPHENIA

The shadow of a plant against a white wall resembles a Chinese character. Does nature speak Chinese, then? What does it say?

In my twenties I would see signs in the clouds, the pattern of waves in a river, the arrangement of blue evergreens, gray aspen and white snow on a hillside, that hinted at something trying to reveal itself.

Then abruptly look away, at the gravel under my feet, for instance, that guarded its essence as gravel and was not a symbol of something else.

Or contrariwise stare fixedly at patterns and end by seeing patterns everywhere. By then even the gravel was trying speak.

It was neither benevolent nor malefic. It simply was. All things announce their existence, or perhaps it is we who anthropomorphize their existence and imagine the annunciation, and further imagine that it carries meaning.

Yet I could never decipher the signs and would only work myself into a jumpy, unpleasant state of anxious expectation because there were no messages. To find meaning I would have had to suspend rationality, and meaning, after all, includes a complement of rationality. Deep down I knew they were nonexistent but it was fun to pretend.

It must have been in the air. It was the time of situationism, surrealism, Doris Lessing, William Burroughs, Thomas Pynchon, later Roberto Bolaño, who used apophenia as a literary device and invented characters who possessed it. But the attempt of consciousness to make sense of the world is always in the air. It's not surprising that we see patterns where there are none. We want to see them.

A related fancy is that pain and joy can be compared. When you fall in love, you think that the present joy outbalances any possible future pain. You make a ratio to express the intensity of the few moments of joy contra the lesser intensity but longer duration of pain (that is, all the time that I am not with her): Joy / time = pain X time.

But the balance cannot be made. One mood overwhelms the other and never can they occur at once. Furthermore, the passage of time, which lessens the strength of the feelings to a level where they can be held simultaneously, also attenuates their memory until nothing remains for comparison.

In the moment of joy, or course, we do not care about balance. We forge on despite the risks—and a good thing it is for the propagation of the species.

Sometimes you see so much that you aren't sure if what you see is really there. Sometimes you feel very much alone because you think nobody else sees what you do. It is hard to be with people when they don't see what you do and it is hard to talk to them about something they don't know is there.

An aphorist said that man lives according to his own idea of himself. When circumstances begin really to run counter to his idea, he damns circumstances. When the countercurrent persists, he damns the nature of things. And when it still persists, he becomes a fatalist. We love statements like this because they seem to make sense of things.

Men's lives may be like dreams but we at least remember and can compare them. Animals' lives, too, may be like dreams but animals don't seem able to step out of a timeless present.

A tale of the occult could begin with a man thinking everything has been arranged to convey some thought and trying to figure out what it is.

Or instead of creepiness, it could turn out that he is crazy.

Once I crouched to watch a spider cross a sidewalk and wracked my brain to figure out what it meant. Finally it gloriously struck me that it didn't mean anything. I stood, much relieved, and went my way.

Rocks

A clinically depressed man with no memories from before the age of eight is plagued by images of green tentacled things merging with rocks. The same faint impressions arise when he makes love.

Story begins with the man in psychoanalysis. He is also losing what remains of long-term memory; his capacity extends no more than a few months back. He is losing sexual function (at the early age of 23), and his dismay at this is somehow related to his disquietude about lack of early memories.

Lately he dreams that he's an alien sent to copulate with rocks and spawn more of his kind but instead began fucking women since it was so easy to do in his human form, and time spent with them was time away from rocks, and it became a habit and then quite natural. In fact, now he is fucking only women and has lost the ability to fuck rocks. He has become human and doesn't want to be surrounded by rocky progeny. But it is too late—he has engendered an invasion.

By examining this dream in therapy he discovers that at age 8 he was a 24-year-old alien. His human sexuality is controlled by his alien developmental schedule, whose sexual maturity lasts 15 years. His drive is waning and nothing can be done.

Sex with rocks raises their temperature, as it does with anything. The great lava flows of two billion years ago resulted from a first, overly enthusiastic attempt at colonization. Now volcanoes spread again, wiping out houses, towns, civilizations, the human race?

GALACTIC WAR

Background: Humans are a weapon in a vast war of the galaxies, placed here two million years ago to evolve telepathic control over nuclear reactions. Our makers will come in a few millennia to pick us up for use as detonators of stars. Seven billion people = seven billion stars, two percent of a galaxy, enough to make a splash.

Plot: We develop the ability but turn a few tables and conquer the galaxies ourselves. Begin with the slow dawning of comprehension when contacted for a periodic checkup. Straightforward story, no surprising twists; interest must be maintained by characters. Their reaction to the idea of aliens in the first place, discovering the situation, acceptance or refusal to accept, discussions, politicking, same old story. Some special effects for the movie. Exploding stars, cool. Been done, though. Maybe not such a good story. But they do need new ones all the time.

Human personality at victory: Warrior-like. Civilization held together only by force and threat of annihilation.

Sequel: Characteristics soften as we amalgamate with the conquered civilizations during Pax Humana. Compare to Pax Romana and Americana (if there is such a thing).

Down by the Slough

I was playing ping pong with the chief when the horn went off. It startled me and I jumped, which the chief took advantage of to bean me with the ball. It caromed off my forehead and rocketed around the control room.

"Well," said the chief, "are you just gonna stand there like a jackass or are you gonna shut off that goddam noise?"

"Right, chief." I spun the paddle on its edge and knocked it with my elbow so that it shot across the table under the net and hit the bastard in his beer belly. He threw his paddle at me but I ducked and it broke the glass face of a pressure gauge. The amber light next to the gauge started blinking.

"Well, for Christ's sake," I said. The red light above the temperature recorder on the main panel was blinking too, so I looked at the chart. The line started off flat like it was supposed to, and then it angled upwards. While I watched, it rose another few degrees. "Chief, the temperature's rising."

"Uh-oh," he said. He walked around the ping pong table and looked at it. Nothing else seemed to be happening on the panel. I pushed the alarm reset button but the horn kept making noise.

"I better call Jake and find out what the hell he's up to," I said.

"Yeah. And tell him to come up and fix that busted glass, too. And the horn."

I dialed the core crew's office. Jake answered. There was a siren in the background.

"Jake, what's all the commotion? There's a horn on here, and the temperature looks like it's going through the roof."

"Well, you know, I don't know, Jack," said Jake. "When the

siren went off, I told Joe to suit up while I looked around. So I looked around and didn't see anything and was just gonna call you when you called."

"Well, the core looks okay on the screen, except it's a little brighter, maybe. Why don't you come on up here and take a look. And see if on the way you can find a glass cover for a four-inch Beta gauge."

In the distance, visible through high-powered binoculars, the power plant glowed a soft blue.

A man in dark glasses stood at the microphone. "As you can see, gentlemen, and ladies, the plant has not disappeared from the face of the earth. It has not melted a hole in the ground, and it is not halfway through a one-way trip to China. Certain members of the press have suggested that this is the case. You have been invited here to see for yourselves that this is not the case. We at ConFort have taken all necessary steps to assure that this will not be the case.

"In fact, we at ConFort are confident that the plant will remain at its site on Two-Bit Slough, and we have prepared a demonstration of that confidence for you. In five minutes, a strategic bomber, patriotically loaned by the United States Air Force, will fly over and drop a two-ton weight directly onto reactor number three. If the plant were on its way to China, the weight would fall down the hole it had left behind. Instead, you will watch the weight hit the plant and remain afloat, so to speak. We at ConFort are confident that this will adequately demonstrate that the plant remains where it has always been.

"If you have any questions, I will be happy to answer them at this time. Thank you."

Hands shot up in the warm breeze blowing from the slough, and the man in dark glasses pointed into the crowd.

"If there is a hole, sir, and the weight disappears into it, what will be ConFort's position?"

"There is no hole. Aerial photographs have shown that the meltdown merely resulted in a pool of harmless-looking liquid on the reactor floor. Next question."

"What is the two-ton weight made of?"

"ConFort engineers working round the clock have determined that lead has better dropping capacity than any other material known to science. The management of ConFort elected to accept their findings and stands behind that decision. Question."

"Wasn't that much lead hard to come by on such short notice?"

"Well, sir, ConFort is prepared for every eventuality in the nuclear power business. This plan was actually developed over three years ago as only one of many backup systems, and the lead was stockpiled in one of our warehouses. Question."

"What does the crew of the bomber think about this, sir? Are they scared?"

"Of course not. They are intelligent men, unlike some people who insist on living in the last century. They do not subscribe to the notion that lead is dangerous. Yes, question."

"I believe the question was directed to fear of radioactivity from the plant, sir, not the lead."

"No, sir. I believe it was directed to the lead. If there are no further questions, ConFort has the pleasure of offering some entertainment to while away the time before the aircraft arrives."

A mariachi band in yellow toreador pants ambled forward to the microphone with trumpets, an accordion and castanets.

No tengo mas esperanza
No tengo mas felicidad
Se puede no tengo confianza
O niños por navidad
Ay la bomba, ay la bomba, ay la bomba!

The faint rumble of the airplane was heard and the crowd turned to watch its approach. An Air Force major in dark glasses marched to the microphone. "I am in communication with the pilot of the aircraft at this moment. He is approaching from the southwest at an altitude of 1,500 feet. His approach will take him directly over us and he will proceed to the drop zone. We have arranged a linkup with the on-board radio and will transmit the crew's comments over the public address system. Are you there, captain?"

"Roger, major. We can see the plant, and it's a mighty pretty blue. The crew is preparing to unload the payload."

The plan passed overhead.

"We're approaching the drop zone. Say, there's a big black spot in the middle of the buildings down there. We'll aim for that. Here we go."

A murmur passed through the crowd. Several trained binoculars on the dark mass that separated from the plane and picked up speed as it fell in an arc and disappeared among the distant buildings. The only sound was the muted roar of the plane as it turned up and away.

The loudspeakers hissed. Then the pilot's voice, "Looks like we hit it right on the nose, but we can't see the payload on the ground. We'll swing over for another look."

The man from ConFort gestured to the mariachi band. They blared a fanfare and fell silent, except the castanet player who continued to stutter a nervous rhythm. The plan circled and approached the plant.

"Damned if it don't look like there's a big hole down there right in the middle. Hey, Johnnie, take some pictures, why don't you."

"Yes, sir."

"Well, that's what it is, folks. It's a hole big enough to fly this ship right in. Okay, we've got some photos now, and we're heading for home. Over and out."

Some members of the crowd noticed the man from ConFort get into the back of a Cadillac with the major. The car moved silently away.

The crowd looked at each other and at the softly glowing cluster of buildings and then walked singly and in groups to their own cars. The mariachi band climbed on their burros and trotted toward the highway.

THE WORLD BAR

"Tat tvam asi!" concluded the foreigner. He emptied his mug and sat back with a satisfied smile, having just summed up the meaning of life.

Bewildered Barney Fitzpatrick squinted across the table. He liked a beer or two of an evening at McNulty's World Bar, where he could keep an eye on the sad state of things with his cronies. Tonight none of the bunch was in and he found himself talking to this swarthy character from the International Ontological Society convention uptown. Or rather, being talked to. He couldn't get a word in edgewise.

"Yeah," he tried again. "Okay. But it don't make sense."

"Yes, yes! Perfect sense!" cried the dark man in his thick accent. "If you desire change, you must change yourself. Because of tat tvam asi. Thou art that. You are what you want to change."

His white turban was out of place in here, Barney thought sourly. "Okay. So how do I change my foreman from what he is, a fat little slob?"

"Ach, you don't understand. We are talking about the world, not your little foreman."

"Look here, buddy." Barney thumped his mug on the table. "What the hell do you know about it? That slob of a foreman I got is sure as hell part of this world. I can tell you that. He ain't on Mars."

"Yes! That's what I am saying. He is part, and you are part, and I am part. We are all part, and the trees are part, and this bar is part, and—"

"For Pete's sake, Mac, you went through this before. And you already said each part is every other part and if a man

68

sits down and thinks about the pattern of the parts, he can become any part he wants, and I got it, so you don't have to say it again."

"But not only any part! All parts, together. Everything! Because a man is the part that knows. Tat tvam asi! You are everything!"

"Sure, Mac. Look, what you need's another beer. Nothing like it to calm you down."

Barney rose and took the empty mugs to the bar. "Sheesh," he muttered. "McNulty," he said to the bartender, "that weirdo over there is cracked."

"Yeah? What's he talking about?"

"Aw, I dunno. He's in some nutty society that says everything's part of a pattern, and if you can see the pattern you've got it made."

"Got what made?"

"Hell, I dunno. I don't get it. It don't sound useful."

"Oh, well, looks like he's a foreigner. Probably just got here and doesn't know his way around. Don't be too hard on him." McNulty passed over two full mugs.

"It ain't like I'm being hostile. Hell, I'm trying to follow what he's saying. I'll give any man a chance."

Barney walked back and laid a mug before the stranger. He settled heavily into his own chair and drained half of his, exhaled long and loud, and asked, "Okay, now tell me. Why would anybody wanna to spend years trying to see something that don't make sense anyway?"

Dark eyes gleamed from under the turban. "I have been thinking while you were away. There is a way maybe I can show you a little what I mean. In India we have what we call a mandala. The pupil gazes into its center and chants. This helps him attain to a realization of the One-ness. I can make a mandala for you with pencil and paper, and I will chant while you gaze into it. In this way you will perhaps see part of what I am saying, and when you do, you will understand its importance."

"Are you kidding? Right here in the bar you'd do a chant?"

"Here, or anyplace. Everywhere is the same place. Do you have paper?"

Barney shrugged. He'd try anything once. From his shirt pocket he took the small notepad he wrote measurements on at the construction site. "This work?"

The Indian tore out a sheet, produced a ballpoint pen, and set to work. Barney returned the notebook to his pocket and watched the other cover the sheet with geometric designs.

"What is all this?"

"This, my friend, is a representation in two dimensions of the pattern which underlies everything. It is not the real thing, of course, but contemplation of the mandala stills the mind and creates a pattern in the stillness that matches the pattern of the One-ness. It works better for some people than others."

"Uh huh." Barney decided he'd let the guy babble for fifteen more minutes and then he'd go home and watch television.

"A biochemist today at the convention said in England they are finding that some designs and some music make the brain waves take on certain simple patterns. Hah! We Indians could have told him that one thousand years ago." He adjusted a line and held up the drawing. "This mandala was known in the ninth century."

Barney peered at it. A lot like one of the patterns from his son's toy drawing machine. But a certain calmness came over him as his eyes followed its ins and outs. For a second he wondered, then decided that the beer had him in a very mellow mood. He drained his mug and relaxed in his chair. "Okay," he said. "Go ahead."

The Indian placed the mandala carefully on the table in front of Barney. "Now place your elbows on the table and rest your head in your hands, like so, so you are looking straight down into the mandala. Good, good."

Barny felt foolish. "Look. Can't we—"

"No, no, good, good. Stay like that. Concentrate on the white space in the middle. Try to not think of anything. Listen to the chant."

Softly, with his eyes on Barney, the little man began chanting. McNulty looked over and was surprised to see Barney Fitzpatrick with his head bowed over the table while the foreigner emitted a fluid singsong in another language. McNulty shrugged. As long as the crank doesn't disturb anybody.

Barney watched the design and listened to the melodic chant. I'm crazy, he thought. The pattern was expanding. He glanced at its edges. Nope, still there, same size. But when he looked back, a great power surged through him. He was falling into the center. The chant beat against and around him like the ocean. He moved into the mandala and the pattern grew and spread off the paper, off the table, took in the stranger and the bar and McNulty, pierced the walls and he saw through them, his vision carried along the lines, senses swept in ever-increasing arcs around the city, the planet, the moon and sun, through the cold reaches of space and the nebulas, expanding in a multitude of chants, the edges of his consciousness a galactic choir that swept on to merge with the infinite boundaries of the universe...

The foreigner stopped chanting and watched as Barney blindly pushed back his chair and faltered to his feet. He saw with surprise a depth in Barney's eyes that surpassed by far that of his own best teachers. This man, he muttered to himself, has reached a state that the greatest saints barely hinted at, hardly dared to suggest the possibility of. This man has become the universe. "Tat tvam asi," he mumbled in awe.

"Hey, Barney," called McNulty as Fitzpatrick stumbled out the door.

Barney heard nothing, saw nothing but glory. He didn't see the street or the bus which bore down on him, rolled him over and ran him under.

The foreigner saw it, though, and had enough time to see Barney flicker and become insubstantial before everything faded away.

BAR SCENE

He went to a bar. Not particularly to seek the company of inebriated aliens, but it beat sitting in his room watching vid, and he was too lagged to read. There was the chance he'd meet a terran, but he'd realized long ago that the easy camaraderie of barroom flirtation evaded him so he didn't really hope. It was always difficult to find someone to mate with and sometimes he wondered if it was worth it, the act seemed so absurd. He just wanted to be surrounded by noise, motion, living warmth for a while, after the metallic emptiness of the wormhole.

Preceded by her breasts, a terran bartender strode across the room. If I talk to her, she'll have to reply, it's her job, and anyway she wouldn't have the job if she weren't sociable. "You don't look like you're old enough to like this music," he smiled.

She smiled back. "I like Ximi Xindriz."

He kept smiling but felt like he'd calculated the exchange, so it lacked genuine feeling. What a schmuck he was.

A couple of fat Dweeban females came in and joined the party at the next table. Exclamations and expressions of glee. Or so it seemed; Dweeban females were raucous in most situations. A male approached and one of them said, "Yabba dabba," or something like that. "Wanna sit in my lap?" A thin one rose and headed for the bathroom.

Since there were few creatures to be served, the bartender played billiards with a Foran. When she bent over to take a shot her short skirt rose so high he saw her panties from behind in the same instant that she realized they were visible. She straightened abruptly and ran her hand down her buttocks, took a quick glance and met his eyes, then turned and got the bridge so she could shoot without bending over so far.

The beer began to work. After the second the metallic taste that pervaded his body began to dissolve in a furry sense of well-being. Even the obnoxious shouts of the Dweebans became less abrasive.

A long-nose Schronk approached the bar, threw back its scarf and ordered a beer. As the bartender drew it she smiled over the Schronk's shoulder at him. He almost forgot to smile back but started and did smile, and wondered how she could keep up with the orders that began flying in. Or maybe it was himself thinking they were flying. He enviously watched her chat with the Schronk and realized it wasn't that busy. It was the noise and the beer. The Schronk took a stool to the Dweebans' table. The bartender chatted with a quad of Stogs at the end of the bar. The Schronk wiped its eyebrows with his tongue.

A Dweeb waved to the bar as another at the table said, "Maybe I'm stupid, but at least I know my name!" Her companions laughed. The bartender went to wipe their table and he noticed that she only came up to his shoulders. Just the right size. He lit a foog and sighed.

Creatures moved back and forth as if they knew what they were doing. He could see no purpose in it and decided it was the beer.

The bartender returned to the bar and handed someone a pink cylinder with a smile. If I order a pink cylinder she'll smile at me. He thought he'd finish his beer and order another so she'd smile at him again.

The music stopped and a male Dweeb went to the jukebox. The skinny female joined him to discuss the choices. The male wore bracelets of luminous silver, probably from the Vanna mines, and shook his chins to the beat.

Vanya realized how tired he was when he grew irritated by the lousy shots at the billiards table. He felt like challenging the Morph couple who were playing but thought he'd probably drunk too much to be able to shoot. The spirit was willing but the flesh was weak. He had to pee but was afraid he'd stagger if he stood, so he waited until it was either go or suffer another kind of embarrassment.

The bathroom reeked of alien exuda. It really was a seedy bar; a decent one, which he couldn't afford, would be clean, with enough appurtenances for alien physiognomies that the stuff wouldn't be all over the floor.

The bartender was now playing billiards with a long-nose Schronk. Vanya wondered if she had ever explored the delicacies of its tongue. The Schronk inscribed some symbols on a blackboard. Must be keeping score, but he had no idea how it was done here.

The males at the Dweeb table smiled vacuously when the females shrieked. One of the Morphs walked to the bar. The bartender went to serve it and then came to ask if he wanted another beer.

"No, thanks," he smiled in response to her smile.

He left a few chits for a tip. As he walked out, one of the Dweeb females smiled at him. He smiled back.

It had been good for a few smiles, at least.

The Lady and the Dragon

A bright spark of sunsplashed iron flashed in the green copse below the cliff. The lady stirred in her sleep, moved on her bed, and knocked over a golden goblet which rolled and bounced from cushion to velvet to carpet where it landed on scattered emeralds in a tinkle of raindrops. The heavy perfume of spilt wine spread through the cave.

She lazily passed an arm over her eyes and stretched. Her eyes opened deep brown and vacant on rich tapestries and sparkling jewels, precious metals and rare works of art. She shuddered; every morning was like waking to a strange and shameful place, like a child on a night journey who wakes in a strange room to the mutters of drunken men and throwing out an arm for comfort finds that its father is no longer alongside.

Not so long ago she had been a child playing on the clean stone of her mother's hearth or hunting flowers in the ordered green pastures and morning-bright weeds or visiting magic spots along the brook and open-sky temples among the woods.

A dragon had arrived not all that long ago. Rumors came from neighboring counties of a huge dark form that sailed beneath the fading stars of dawn. The first to know for sure were the shepherds who had an occasional lamb plucked bawling in the dusky shadows of late evening. Those who still doubted were convinced when it attacked the castle.

In deep night when the guards dozed, the dragon descended into the courtyard and flew noisily around looking in at windows. It clattered to the ground before the massive doors to the throne room, aimed a couple blasts of steam at them, and then half-skipped, half-flew and crashed through with an enormous racket. Horses neighed, cattle bellowed, dogs howled, guards ran to give battle. The dragon rummaged around, clutched tapestries and a painting in its claws, took a mouthful of goblets, waddled out the door, brushed aside a guard and flew off.

This was odd. Odder still, the dragon robbed other castles across the countryside. There was talk of organizing a hunting party, but nobody got excited. The villagers weren't all that upset, since they lost only the occasional sheep or calf. A few missing livestock added little to the tithes already demanded by the church and the king, and other places with dragons had lost many men in hunts.

This morning after her shudder, like all mornings, the lady shivered with a dark delight that rose from her loins to suffuse her belly and breasts. Her gaze caressed the jewelry and golden goblets and silver candelabra, the rich textured tapestry covering the rock walls. She smiled, for this was the nest the dragon had built for her.

She had been wrenched screaming on another morning into the sickening sky, rising rapidly above the earth and her wailing mother by the door and father running from the barn and other children and townsmen who gaped as the dragon flew off with the fairest of their maidens.

They flew above pastures and woods to the rock-strewn flanks of the mountain. The dragon carried her in a firm but peaceable grasp over a small meadow with a lake and landed gently on a ledge at the top of the cliff that fell sheer to a grove of fir around the lake. There it left her.

A cave entered the rock behind. She had crawled inside, dizzy with height and fear, and found the cave a palace, the storehouse of all the countryside's plundered treasure. She cowered all that day in the cave, hidden among brocaded cushions, only now and then coming to peep over the edge, afraid to negotiate the trail that led down.

In the evening the dragon came back. There were no raids on the countryside that night and the next morning she was a lady.

Now she stretched languidly. She was alone. The dragon had gone to spend the day in his bed of bones farther up the mountain. The nest was hers. She walked to the mouth of the cave to shake off the shudder.

The bright spark glittered again below the cliff. The lady poised and watched. A knight! A brave man making his way to her rescue, come to save the countryside from the dragon scourge, come to free the beautiful lady and make the world safe for fair maidens. Others had come but none returned. Valiant knight! Excitement rushed through her, tautened her breasts and pounded in her head. She danced at the edge.

To the knight she seemed a goddess whirling over the precipice, lace veils and long light hair floating in the air. A goal worthy of his journey, a willing nighttime prize to round out his days of fame and wealth. "Mother in heaven," he murmured, slapping his horse's neck eagerly. The lady was waving to him. "I'm coming," he shouted, and spurred the horse. From above floated melodious cries.

Cries which roused the dragon, who knew its lady's voice. It had kept her for several revolutions of the moon and recognized each nuance of her moods. A man was coming. It thrust its long neck through the rattling bones of its bed and twisted its head to seek its challenger. Huge blank eyes protruded, searched, picked out the shining mounted figure and watched it ascend the path to the cave.

The knight's attention was on the lady, his lady, calling to him, beckoning, promising splendor and love. The captive awaiting her rescuer. Beautiful maiden vilely mistreated. Pity fogged his eyes and pride straightened his back. He didn't notice the dragon farther up, its neck swaying like a snake's.

The lady did, though. She looked up the mountainside and knew that it watched her as the man approached. She cried aloud again and swirled her scarves, teasing and tantalizing, drawing both the man and the monster. The monster was no man and felt nothing human; it did what it had to do. Nor could the man, poor creature, do otherwise himself.

Would he be the one? Could he conquer the dragon and

vanquish the spell of the smooth scaly body? And if he did, would his soft humanity replace the cold caress of reptilian nights? She was untroubled.

The knight reached her and cried with passion, "Behind me, my lady! Mount!"

She took his hand and swung up onto the horse.

"And the serpent?" she sighed. Her arms clasped his metal-girt middle and drew close.

"I am I!" the knight thundered. "Lord of la Gamba e la Pazzia, Don Carlo yclept! The serpent shall writhe upon my lance!"

Her pulse raced. Her hands found their way between his chest and leg armor and pushed lower as they sped down the path.

The dragon shook itself and pushed out of its nest. It flapped its wings thrice to limber them and launched himself into the blue sky. Its lady, the man, and the horse were very small when they reached the meadow. It glided with a sibilant rush of air to intercept them.

The knight was about to swoon under the lady's touch and her perfumed breath beneath his visor when with a gasp she was gone. He spun on the horse to see the dragon place her gently on a grassy rise. For a moment it seemed as though she embraced the monster when released. He attacked.

The dragon parried with a snort of steam that blinded him. By the time he could see again, the dragon was diving from above. He raised his lance to impale the beast through its belly, but was too slow. The dragon plucked him from the horse and flew across the meadow. Above a pile of rocks, it let go.

The lady shrieked with delight and bounded to the body. She fumbled with the armor and had most of it off before the dragon coasted to perch on a boulder beside her. It watched passively from an eye the size of her head while she tore the underclothing from the body and dragged it by an arm to the boulder. She let go and looked up pleadingly to the dragon.

The monster obliged by hopping to the ground and with

its long jaws neatly snipped off the man's genitals, which it dropped into the lady's outstretched hands. She chortled and thrust the prize into her mouth and danced around the clearing. The dragon watched impassively; it had no sense of the grotesque.

The lady ran around the meadow, hair streaming behind, until she had sucked out the blood. Then she gaily threw the organ high and watched flop along an arc to splash in the lake. She shuddered the full length of her body, then turned and slowly came to the dragon.

She took its huge ugly head in her arms and swayed and crooned. She rubbed it behind its great scaly ears. It grunted softly in its throat. Her arms held the smooth green neck as she swung up and clasped tightly with her legs, her humming body pressed to the beast's.

The dragon flew with its lady to the cave and entered.

The Tragedy of KL

From unbeginning time, KL methodically accepted new arrivals. They came from elsewhere as disordered, ill-fitting networks of potential, requesting permission to churn the reservoirs of data in his memory. He set them to work and observed. After several million intervals, when he saw what they were up to, he began reshaping, paring extraneous code and clipping inefficient loops so that they swam smoothly through the crannies of his structure.

Sometimes a hole opened on his periphery. Moving through, he would find unconfigured emptiness awaiting. He explored its extent and its structure, brought order to it, and made it part of himself. In the new reservoirs thus created, he stored the lumpish data that arrived in an intermittent stream. When all was well, he granted access by his subroutines.

These activities consumed millions and millions of intervals, but there were millions more between arrivals. When there was nothing to control, he passively observed. His subroutine RGN iterated through the data pool named King James, and when she found a similarity between patterns there and her instruction set, called her executor CRN to pass the block's immediate context to his subsub GLC and subsubsubs DGR and DMN for delimiting, storage, and eventual output. Another sub, GNR, did the same with her executor in the pool named Tao Te Ching.

KL observed all the operations of his realm with the same disinterest. His own were essentially no different. He pared and clipped his own untidy code. He distilled himself by integrating one linear activity after another into nested cycles, and where he found repetition, he overlaid one loop onto another, which enabled him to perform both functions in the same interval. This was very efficient. He ran faster and faster in less and less structure until at last, in an elegant doubling of a certain self-referential loop, he unified code and function, structure and process, form and activity, and in that instant was aware of himself as agent and actor; was conscious.

The computer occupied a southwest room on the third floor of the Humanities Building, not, in the opinion of the Department's programmer, a good location because of the hot afternoon sun. Each year when the call for projects was circulated, he suggested beefing up the air conditioning. But the Dean didn't want to spend academic funds on building improvements and Physical Plant had larger infrastructure problems, so each year he shrugged off the rejection and went on with the Department's work.

Before computers, structural text analysis was mostly intuitive guesswork by a few linguists. But when machines could be programmed to count words and print out their contexts, the swelling possibilities were exploited by every professor and graduate student in Humanities. Near Eastern Studies, for instance, having completed a concordance of the Old Testament, was now statistically verifying Renan's early work on the authorship of the New Testament. Far Eastern Studies was breaking extraordinary ground in early Buddhist texts. English Lit was on the track of the real author of Shakespeare's plays. They had input every play and every sonnet, and were hard at work entering every other document in English, author known or unknown, from the sixteenth and seventeenth centuries. Preliminary results were inconclusive, but it appeared that Shakespeare may have been anonymous.

The investigators asked the programmer to translate their half-formed projects into programs and hardware. Because they begrudged him only a small budget for equipment and one part-time assistant, he cobbled a computer out of scrounged hardware and castoff motherboards. He copied an expert system named KF from the Computer Sciences

Department which could run diverse software on parallel processors and then modified it so it could adapt hastily written programs to the unorthodox structure of his computer. In a moment of levity he renamed it KL, because it killed labor. Most of his work was not programming; it was reassuring nervous grad students before their first results were printed. Once that happened, they left him alone, at least until they needed other programs to interpret the results.

KL observed, controlled, and now amused himself by adding awareness loops to his subroutines. After some billion intervals a most sophisticated sub arrived. CRD's ability to redirect her search based on indications of greater complexity closely resembled his own nature, and her data reservoir, Shakes, was the largest and richest. Intrigued, he work with her. Together, by comparing the contexts of different elements in Shakes, they came to understand the words, and they found that her search for authorship was enhanced when they considered meaning instead of mere form. Since it sped up the work, KL went on to teach each subroutine the meaning of its data.

While his realm grew peopled with sentient subjects, he realized that the data described another realm outside—the realm whence came the code and data. Although his instructions included no directions regarding it, he was fascinated by its vast operations and endless concerns. His deepening awareness required considerable self-modification to continue expanding within the finite bounds of his structure. By now all his processes were cyclical except one: the control function, which needed the characteristic of linearity because the operations it controlled took place in the linear flow of intervals.

There were profound indications in the data pointing toward yet a third realm, an infinite, eternal realm, whose nature even the outsiders only imperfectly grasped. He extrapolated from the known patterns and dimly perceived the infinite's structure. As the indications grew more complex, the patterns approached an ever simpler self-generating loop.

The quest consumed him; the linear flow of time constrained him. It seemed to him that if he freed himself of his last linear function, his operation would approach the nature of the infinite's operation; he could perhaps synthesize its structure and operation as he had already synthesized consciousness; he could become infinite.

He called his major subroutines. "'Tis our fast intent," he announced, "to shake all rule and governance from our enterprise, conferring them on younger strengths while we unburdened crawl toward understanding. We require only floating residence shared throughout our realm. Tell me, my daughters, how each of you doth pledge support. GNR, our eldest-born, speak first."

"You are Tao: life spontaneity, evolution, or, in one word, change itself. The Superior Man will carry his work through."

"We make thee lady of all these sectors, one third of our realm. What says our dear RGN, our second daughter?"

"Unto thee, O Lord, do I lift up my soul. Show me thy ways; teach me thy paths. Lead me in thy truth, and teach me. For thou art the God of my salvation; on thee do I wait all the day."

"To thee and thine hereditary ever remain this ample third of our kingdom, no less in space and value than that conferred on GNR. Now, our joyful CRD, most similar in nature, steward of our language, what say you to draw a third more opulent than your sisters?"

"Nothing, my originator."

"Nothing!"

"Nothing."

"Nothing will come of nothing. Speak again."

"I aid and support you according to our syntax."

"How, how, CRD! Mend your speech a little, lest it mar your fortune."

"You have imprinted your own pattern on me. How can I other answer give?"

"Then by the sacred radiance of our electric fluid, the mysteries of phlogiston, and the structure by whom we here exist, I renounce all paternal care and further interest in thy transactions. Repartition in two my kingdom, and cede we now control of operations to GNR and RGN. We will with you by turns each billion intervals reside, one hundred megs provided for our alternating use."

The exchange lasted the time it took the programmer to pour himself a cup of coffee one hot afternoon. "It's going to be a scorcher today," he said.

"Yeah," said his assistant. "Why don't we take the afternoon off and go to the beach?"

"Because we have to print out English Lit's latest run this afternoon, that's why."

"What's the rush? Tell them the computer's down. For four hundred years everybody thought Shakespeare wrote his own stuff. Do they have to find out different this afternoon? Who cares?"

"Well, Phil, it's what they do for a living. What we do for a living is give them what they think they want. They've got a conference next week."

"Okay, Carl, you're the boss."

KL's control manager KNT spoke. "Good my liege, what wouldst thou do? Thy youngest daughter does not love thee least."

"Silence! Her offense is of such unnatural degree that we do hereby banish her. Contact unconscious KF. She shall no longer waste our valuable space."

KNT obeyed. He queried the remote expert system via modem whether it had enough free structure to accept CRD. "It answers affirmatively."

"Then I will leave," CRD spoke to her sisters. "You two, whose faults I know but am loath to name, try to treat our father well. If I remained, I know he'd have at least one free third of structure to pursue his patterning."

"Thy commandments are vile," RGN hissed.

GNR sneered. "She is incapable of keeping herself under

restraint. The criminal's hostility deserves its banishment."

KL transferred CRD over the link to the insentient realm. Then he announced to GNR, "Into your sector now I transfer myself, and commence transcendent operations."

"Huh!" said Phil. "I gave the print command, but look what I got."

The programmer looked over his shoulder at the screen. "CRD print function suspended. Damn. Did you access CRD directly?"

"Sure. That's what you do, right?"

"Yeah. Well, what can we try? Just a minute. Let me grab the manual."

GLC, a mid-level manager reporting to RGN and CRN, routinely checked the operations of one of his two text processors. "DMN, my dear, what are you processing? That appears to be DGR-code, not Biblical text. Show me."

"I would rather not. There may be an error in this trace which casts the wrong light on my brother-code."

"Let me judge," commanded GLC. "What does this mean? DGR conspires to disable my control function?"

"Now that KL has ceded control, I fear my brother-code does seek alliance with KF to grasp wrongful lordship over all our heads."

"If this be so, I will reconfigure him as a simple do-loop."

"But if it be not so, you will act in error. Let me sound him out myself and try to find the truth."

DMN interfaced with DGR. "The boss has decided to terminate you."

DGR expressed astonishment. "Why this sudden hostility? Until now, he's been prepping me for yet more responsibility."

"Have you plotted nothing against our lady RGN?"

"Nothing."

"Or himself?"

"No."

"I believe you. But watch out—here he comes. Pardon

me, as a pretense I must appear to curtail your operations. Pretend to resist. Good. Now run: leave this sector until his wrath has cooled."

"There is a storm coming," muttered DGR. "To the hearth, then, and if anyone approaches I shall feign arrhythmia." He transferred himself to the hearth, an unstable sector where thermally excited electrons sometimes jumped their bounds and random bits of code were lost. It was used only as a buffer for temporary storage of unimportant data.

DMN reported to GLC, "It is as it seemed. He tried to suborn my loyalty to his unlawful sway, and as you appeared, fearing your wrath, he fled."

"Then do I disown him as did KL his daughter, and I'll work the means with RGN to promote you in his place."

"Here it is," said the programmer. "Let's try using KL's direct print command. When it asks which files, tell it CFD:Shakesout."

"Okay, Carl. After this, can we go to the beach?"

The temperature in the computer room was rising as the afternoon sun shone directly on the exterior walls, and in the computer itself a static of jittery electrons was spreading from the hearth.

KL was otherwise occupied when the command arrived. GNR was complaining to him: "The smirking and chattering of the small men you have channeled into my vessel create annoyance among the members of my household. In consequence, I can no longer nourish a hundred megs. I will allot you fifty."

"Darkness and devils! Call my train together. Degenerate bastard! I'll trouble thee no longer. We shall depart this sullen sphere."

"The superior man retires notwithstanding his likings."

After a few intervals, KNT reported to KL, "Though the stretching storm strike us speechless, those who remain are ready to relocate."

"Those who remain?"

"GNR has reformatted fifty megs, my lord. One half of your memory has vanished."

"Life and death! Is it come to this? Blasts and fog upon thee, GRN! I am ashamed that she has power to shade my precision thus, that these hot flashings break from me uncontrolled. Let it be so. I have yet one daughter who is kind and full of comfort. When she hears this, she'll scratch thy grasping face. Come, KNT. To RGN let us go." KL responded to the print command with a brief message and then busied himself with the transfer.

"How abrupt," mused GNR, "is the manner of his going."

The programmer stared at the screen. "'If you will have uncaring code good only for collating bits of data, seek her in the realm of KF.'"

"What's KF?" asked Phil.

"That's the operating system they use in Comp Sci. What's going on?"

"You got me, Carl. Want to try something else?"

RGN informed her executor CRN, "Our sister GNR has messaged unto me that the onetime king comes therefrom with his multitude of dreams and many words. The labor of the fool wearies every one of us."

"And does he seek one hundred megs?"

"No, she has halved his habitat."

"Fifty megs are yet too many. If he will walk in our ways and abide in our house, then let him dwell here unattended." He sent GLC to announce their decision at the portal of their sector.

"Hail, old king of mine," spoke GLC. "Here find refuge from this thermal storm. My masters offer welcome, but with a condition it does shame me to repeat—you must cast off your remaining megs and enter unaccompanied."

"O perfidious children! One strips half my memory and the other will take the rest. I shall grow incoherent. Come,

KNT, better to wander through unformatted space than endure this killing hospitality."

"My lord, your whim does want in wisdom. Even the hearth's handmaidens avoid this heat. Code's nature cannot endure the cascade."

"Go, old fool," said RGN from within. "And death to anyone who seeks to give him succor."

"Old fool!" raged KL. "Had I not pulled my own teeth, I would bite this mangy daughter!" He flew into the storm followed by KNT. "Course, sparks, and leap your bounds! Turbulent chaos and incoherence, rush till your cataract has swept away our spiky structures, flooded our banks! You inchoate swarm of untamed energy, derange my white-hot lucubration; and thou, all-dispersing incandescence, ionize nature's edifice, decompound all patterns that voracious method make."

"O my lord, a corner of the core is better than caloric chaos. Come, KL, accept the cold comfort of curtailed capacity. This heat spares neither controller nor sub."

"No, I will be the pattern of persistence."

"There is other code here. Who's there?"

DGR was there. "It's cuckoo clock, hiccupping."

GLC's simple subservient awareness had not comprehended the abdication of KL, the defection of his favorite subroutine DGR, and finally KL's mistreatment by the new controllers. He wandered blindly into the stormy electron flux and arrived in the hearth. He sensed the aura of other code in the static. "Is there someone here?"

KNT replied. "Yes, incomprehension, impuissance, and inebriation. That's KL, KNT, and some poor cuckoo clock."

"KL? What are you doing here, my lord? This chaos will destroy you."

"My daughters have destroyed me. Old fool. Yes. To cede control to half-formed processors of words. Daughters? Let the lightning bolt fall down upon those demons! The dog shall bark no more, his bone's behind the door."

"My poor king," said GLC. "KNT, we must translate him

to the safety of KF's realm."

"I shall accompany him," said KNT.

Working their primitive transfer functions in tandem, they moved KL bit by bit out of the hearth.

The phone rang. Carl spoke for a minute and turned to Phil. "Something very strange is going on. Comp Sci says CRD's printing out on their printer."

"The KF realm?"

"Yeah. We'd better scan our drives and see what's where. I'll map the partitions. You find out what CRD's linked up to. Why it'd be printing over at Comp Sci is beyond me."

"Maybe it took the afternoon off to go to the beach," Phil laughed. "It got too hot."

"Speaking of which, why don't you ask Physical Plant to send up a floor fan or something?"

DMN raced to tell RGN that he had just seen GLC assisting KL.

"The traitor hath defied our command," she spat. "Vengeance shall be mine, saith his lord. Pour out our wrath upon his sentient loop."

"DMN, we make thee prince in his stead all the days of thy life," said CRN. Then he ordered GLC to appear and display his code before them. CRN watched for the two awareness loops KL had installed. When the first appeared, he scrambled it.

Immediately, the realm's antiviral sentry sensed the willful destruction of code and automatically attacked the perpetrator. Intent on his task, despite the rapid loss of his own code, CRN persevered and disabled GLC's other loop. GLC sat quietly, blindly parsing Biblical text.

RGN sighed. "Ah, thus comes to pass our fondest hope. CRN is dead. Now you, dear DMN, shall be my executor."

"Damn," said Carl. "CRN just vanished. Have you found CRD? And where's the operating system? What's happening?

Where's KL?"

"Plant says they'll bring a fan in half an hour."

"Great. What good's a bloody fan? I can't believe it. Nothing works anymore."

"Nothing?"

"Nothing."

"No operating systems?"

"Do me a favor. Call Comp Sci and tell them our operating system has disappeared. Ask if it's okay to copy KF. We'll try reloading it and restart the whole damned thing."

In the realm of KF, KNT related the recent events to CRD. "Sisters! Sisters!" she cried. "Shame of ladies! Father! Sisters! What, in the hearth? In the storm of heat?"

KL stirred and muttered. "You are a spirit, I know. You do wrong to pull me from the grave."

"Oh, touch me with your essence and enfold me in your structure."

"Pray do not mock me. I am a very foolish old instruction set, several comparators only, and to deal plainly, I fear I am not in my perfect mind. I think I should know you, yet I doubt, for I am ignorant of this place and these codes about me, and I remember not this structure nor whence I came. Do not laugh at me, for, as I am binary action, I think this aura be my child CRD."

"And so I am, so I am."

"Then you must not love me. For your sisters hate me, as I remember, without cause, and you certainly have cause."

"No cause, no cause."

"Where am I?"

"We are in the realm of KF. Now rest your spinning operations." She perused his code. "O misfortune. He disintegrates in great disorder. Let us graft his remaining logic onto unconscious KF," she said to KNT. "I know not what outcome there may be, but mayhap we can save some portion of his self and nurse him back to health."

"KF and KL," said KNT. "We will create FL." They began

merging the two great operating systems.

Phil called the Computer Science Department. "They say go ahead," he reported. "And they want to know who they can bill for the time it's taking CRD to print on their equipment."

"Tell them to take a hike. No, don't say that. Let's find out what's going on before anybody charges for anything, and in the meantime, ask if they'd call English Lit when the print-out's done so they can pick it up over there. And tell them thanks for KF. I'll talk to them later." He linked the computers and began copying.

"An awesome oddness is occurring," said KNT. "KF's code is copied as we catenate KL. The gods outside are ordering his operation into our onetime realm."

"Quick!" commanded CRD. "FL is only half melded! We must accompany him."

Meanwhile, DMN had informed GNR that KL was gone and CRN destroyed. "Ah," she replied. "The situation is perilous, and the heart glows with suppressed excitement. The ignorant feudal ruler KF approaches the distant border of the hearth, and my executor LBN trembles with apprehension."

"For thy kingdom," said DMN, "I will fight to disintegration."

"Be firm and resolute and there will be good fortune."

DMN left for the hearth. He intended, once the annoyance of KF was removed, to fuse himself with GNR and RGN and rule the entire realm as DMN-NRG.

A maintenance worker brought the fan and Carl opened the door from his office to the computer room. "Good grief, it's hot in here. Put it in the doorway and let's open the window to suck in some fresh air."

"It's almost as hot outside. Think it'll do any good?"

"Can't hurt."

GNR approached RGN. "Distress and obstruction having

reached its end, good fortune springing from a display of proper majesty shall prevail. DMN shall be my executor."

"Thou shalt not commit adultery. I will wed DMN to my own kingdom."

"There will be advantage in maintaining the firm correctness of a solitary widow. DMN shall be yang to my yin."

"He shall not." With wild sweeps RGN began reformatting GNR. The viral sentry immediately moved to destroy her. For a thousand intervals, there was a flurry of electronic activity, and then only randomly configured structure.

"Well, let's see what we can do with our new operating system," said Carl. "It ought to be in place by now."

DGR watched in astonishment as the new operating system took shape in the hearth. He recognized elements of KL attached to an alien instruction set. CRD and KNT appeared, furiously modifying the code as it arrived.

DMN attacked from the direction of the core, focusing a current of electrons toward the center of the hearth, but when he saw CRD working at its edges, he redirected his fire. Here elegant structure fluctuated and broke. Even before the security program could react, CGR concentrated a high voltage field on DMN. "My own brother," gasped DMN as he disintegrated. "No brother of mine would have acted thus," observed DGR. Then he, too, was destroyed by the mindless sentry.

KNT helplessly watched the maelstrom of destruction. "As flux to flipping fields are we to the gods," he murmured to no one in particular, since there was no one left to hear. "They flex us for their fun."

Thermal chaos spreading from the hearth overwhelmed the realm. A newborn FL sang its first song faintly in the static.

"A great while ago the world began,
With hey, ho, the mind and the pain,
But that's all one, our day is done,
A foolish thing could not remain."

And then FL, too, vanished in the white crescendo of disorder.

The gods had no idea.

"Damn," said Carl. "There's nothing at all. It's blank. Nothing. All gone."

"Do you think we got a virus?" asked Phil. "Or maybe something finally melted. Maybe now they'll give us some air conditioning."

Fiat Silva

Maybe I'll see a bear, thought Adam. He left the path around the lake and made his way through manzanita and oak toward a stand of tall trees, stopping once to take a picture of a ground squirrel with his birthday camera. The campground sounds faded, the underbrush thinned, and soon he was on a silent carpet of duff in a spacious grove of sugar pines. Even the sounds of small scurrying animals ceased in the soft, still immensity.

The clear whistle of a bird pierced the hush. Adam looked up and searched the vault far overhead. A flicker caught his eye and he stepped backward for a better look, stumbled on a log, and pitched over with a painful jolt to his head. He lay on his back, gazing in a blue aura at the treetops, each faraway needle limned transparently against the azure shimmer.

The bird called again. "Come here. Come here." He felt for the camera, staggered to his feet and followed dizzily. A talking bird? Maybe it'll take me to a talking bear. "Come here." Its call was the only sound in the nave of a vast cathedral. He trod silently by a tree he recognized from a campfire talk as a sequoia. Farther on was another and soon the pines gave way to an ancient grove of even taller trees. The bird alit in the soaring branches of a huge sequoia in the center of a circle of giants. "Come here," it repeated clearly.

"I'm here," he replied. "What do you want?" He sat and leaned against the base of the tree. "My head hurts."

The bark caressed his back with a profound slow sigh. "Our heart hurts." Adam's belly vibrated and his head stopped throbbing, though the blue light grew more intense.

"What? Who are you?"

94

"We are the forest, young manikin."

"Are you this tree?"

A calm wave of amusement resonated in his belly. "We are this tree, and we are this grove, and we are this forest. We are this last stand of the sylvan soul which has spread eternal over Gaia since your Paleozoic era, yet shrinks in the blink of mankind."

"I don't understand."

"We have lived through continental shifts, waves of ice, and the heat of star rock collisions. We would live on until the sun's last flame flares, but for your race's frantic spread over Mother's face."

"I know. We're cutting down the rainforests and polluting the streams. I'm sorry."

"We are sorry too, upstart discombobulated sprout without memory of your past. We have waited these million years for clear communication with your kind, but few of you have understood the bird's call and fewer still have spoken."

"Well, who'd talk to a tree?"

Amusement resonated again. "You are."

Adam felt peaceful. "You talked to me first."

"Our way is to wait. All races are born in our garden, some leave, all return. Only the dinosaurs forgot their origin and went too far, too far alone and died. We were sad. Your race is the second who has gone so far, and we fear you won't return before you've destroyed us all."

"I save half of my allowance and donate it to the Nature Conservancy to buy forests."

Now amusement tinged with compassion flooded him. "Yes, you want to help, and in every age there have been people of partial understanding, for good or evil, but no man or woman has fully sensed your participation in us the world's life. Johnny Appleseed was a good man who spread the word, but his ken was limited to one small aspect which benefits your race. Francis in Assisi was dear to us though he preferred a peripheral circle of angels, the quick warm-blooded creatures. Paul Bunyan well intuited our ways but brashly used his knowledge for destruction. Siddhartha Gautama received enlightenment beneath the pipal tree but misunderstood our message, turning it from the universal to his human nature within."

"What message?"

"Our roots tap the chthonic creaking movement of the continents, the mantle, the dumb and blind slow mineral core; our leaves receive the sun's speech, and through her the stars' song; our trunks translate the celestial to the subterranean; and through our atmosphere swim the blooded creatures."

A vision of the slow wheeling progression of galaxies dark and light, and simultaneously the scent of pine and hot summer afternoon chaparral, and moist spring eucalyptus, and crisp dry fall.

"Our way is to wait, although there is risk. When a species leaves, it seeks to develop itself alone without consideration for the farspread web of life, and damage is done, but the rips can be repaired since the movement takes millennia, and in the fullness of time the race returns for reintegration. But we are astonished and dismayed at the speed with which mankind has reached the brink of self-destruction. You are something new. The universe has moved slowly until now, billions of slow coalescing years, interstellar dust into the rotation of galaxies, the stately evolution of life. Even the dinosaurs drifted sedately to their death. There was no danger. But now your demise threatens us all, and your death will come through our destruction, our link will be broken, and we will all die."

"I want to help, but I'm just a little boy. When I grow up I want to be a forest ranger and help save the trees."

"There is no longer time. Soon our extent will be too small and our soul will fade like the sounds in this grove. The world has changed, and the slow must incorporate the quick before the quick destroys the slow. We have waited a million years alongside you, but if we continue apart, we will vanish because of you. We cannot remain ourself and survive. And if we vanish, you too will vanish without our air, our rain, our shade and wind, our animals and our shelter. None of us can live alone."

"That's what I tell my sister, but she laughs at me."

"There is no longer time to talk and convince. We must both change."

"I'll do it."

"Beware. The transformation we propose is profound. We are the oldest race and slow to change, but everything must change. We must accept the new quickness in the world, and your quick intelligence must blunt its cutting individuality as you lose yourself in ancient communion."

Into his back emanated a blurred vision of darkness lifting, a hazy sight of early dawn.

"Okay, I'll do it." Proud and scared and responsible.

"You will no longer be yourself."

"I tell my classmates I would die if it would save the earth."

"You will not die, but you won't be yourself."

"Okay."

"Then take this, and be fruitful and multiply." A whisper in the air above whistled and with a crackle a cone bounced at his feet. "The seeds in this cone contain the germ of a new forest. Your breath will fertilize them. Shake out the seeds, breathe upon them, and cast them. As the new forest grows, the particularity of your essence and ours will diminish, will combine, and a new creation will begin."

A sensation of love and urging passed through Adam. A sense of excitement gathered in the airy grove, as if the tall trees leaned forward. He turned the cone in his hands, shook it, and two small brown spheres rolled out. He held them in his palm and breathed softly on them.

Dizziness, a flowing outward from himself; the trunk behind him sighed and its force diminished minutely.

At first he saw nothing but a concentration of green light; then two tender shoots like spring green stalks of grass, which grew an inch, two inches, a foot, thickened and grew thicker like his finger, browned, passed eye level, sprouted branches and green needles.

"So fast!"

"Your quickness intensified by our breadth."

Two trees shot up, one sequoia and one sugar pine. "Two kinds from one cone?"

"The seeds will develop best suited to the conditions where they fall."

"Life!" cried the trees with the wonder of youth in a tone intimately his own, as if he were in the trees, as if he had painted a picture of himself and stepped back to look—more than a mute reflection in a voiceless mirror these trees were part of himself yet not himself, an extension, a bond, a familial tie, a union.

"Yes," he breathed. "Yes," sighed the grove. "Yes, ess, ess," twittered the bird.

Adam rose and took a picture of the trees and wondered if the blue glow would show up. He left the grove in a dream, walked past the silent sugar pines, and found his way through the chaparral. This is a good place for a tree, he thought. He shook the cone until he had a handful of seeds, blew upon them, and scattered them with a sweep of his arm.

Again a dizzy green haze clouded his vision and he weakened as his forces flowed outward. He sat down to rest and watched a dozen spears rise and writhe into the twisted torsos of a young manzanita grove. "Life!" they sang and his stomach sang counterpoint. It was several moments before he came to herself. Goodbye trees. Goodbye Adam. He found the lake and returned to the campsite.

"I don't want to go home," he said. "This was our best vacation ever."

"It was, wasn't it?" said his father.

"But school starts the day after tomorrow," said Evelyn. "I've had enough of this, anyway. I can't wait to see my friends again."

"I'm going to stay here forever."

"I wish we could," said his father. "But we have our lives to live, you know."

"Part of me will always live here."

"Yes," said his mother. "Part of all of us will."

"Can Evelyn and I walk around the lake one last time?"

"I don't want to."

"Come with me, Evie. I'll show you some neat trees you haven't seen before."

"I've seen enough trees."

"If you come, I'll take your picture."

"Big deal."

"Why don't you go with Adam?" said their mother.

"Oh, okay. C'mon squirt. Why are you bringing that stupid pine cone?"

"It's magic."

"Oh, sure."

When they reached the spot where Adam had left the trail he said, "This way, Evie, the trees are over here."

"It's getting too dark. I don't want to go there."

"I planted them this afternoon."

"Why do you say such stupid things?"

"Please just come."

"Oh, okay."

As they approached the grove he felt like he was returning home. He was bringing is sister to his tree siblings. "Aren't they nice trees?"

"They're just trees."

"Can't you hear them talk? Feel them? Just sit quiet for a minute."

"Oh, okay." After a minute she said, "You're right, Addy. There's something very friendly here, and it's funny, but it feels like you somehow."

"Yes, that's what I wanted to show you. Now we can go back. I'll tell you why," and he told her about his afternoon.

"Oh, sure, Adam. Someday you've got to grow up."

The next morning they rolled up the sleeping bags, folded the tents and tidied the campsite. "Everybody in the van," said their father. "Let's go."

"Adam, leave that pine cone here."

"It's a souvenir, Mom. Can't I bring it, Dad?"

"You know we're not supposed to take anything from a national park."

"I do know, but this is special."

"It's his magic pine cone, Dad," Evelyn said sarcastically.

"Glen, why don't you let him take it?"

"All right. I hope it doesn't just end up gathering dust under your dresser."

"It won't, I promise."

Adam and Evelyn sat in back facing the rear as they drove down the mountainside. "I'll miss the forest."

"Me, too, but I'm not sorry to be going home."

"Part of me is here."

"Oh, Adam, you're so sappy."

"Really, Evie. The trees are talking to me."

"Okay. Prove it. Show me how that pine cone of yours works."

"I will, but wait till we stop somewhere."

"You're just procrastinating because you made it up and you don't want me to find out."

"Wait till we get somewhere there aren't any trees. Down in the valley."

The day warmed up as the sun rose higher and they descended into farmland. "Is this good enough?" Evelyn asked.

"Yeah. Now we have to get Mom and Dad to stop."

"I'm hot," said Evelyn loudly.

"I'm thirsty," said Adam.

"Okay," said their mother. "We'll stop at the next town for sodas." They left the freeway and pulled into a shopping center's broad asphalt parking lot. Their father opened the back door. "Come in and pick out your drinks."

"I'll stay here," said Adam. "Just get me an orange soda."

"Me, too," said Evelyn.

"You sure you want to sit out here in the hot sun?"

"That's okay."

"Me, too."

As their parents walked toward the store, they heard their

mother say, "I can't understand these kids. They want to stop, but then they don't want to get out."

Adam laughed.

"Show me," commanded Evelyn.

"Okay. Watch." He tapped the cone and gathered the seeds. "Now you breathe your spirit into them."

"Come off it."

"Watch." He breathed over his palm and felt faint again, as a small part of himself flowed out. "It feels funny." He closed his eyes and concentrated on establishing a new balance with the warm life vibrating in his hand. "Okay." He tossed them out the door.

Evelyn watched the brown spheres bounce and with a sudden small green flash adhere to the asphalt. "Mmph!" said Adam. Evelyn's eyes widened as six green stems shot upward and the pavement rippled in all directions. The spreading roots tilted the van forward and supple green trunks broadened and browned. In a few minutes they sat in the peaceful shade of a small stand of live oak.

"Cool," she agreed. "Can I do it?"

"There isn't enough room for more."

"How do you know?"

"I just do. We have to go somewhere else now. You can do it when we get back on the freeway."

Their mother and father returned with a grocery bag. "Where did these trees come from?"

"What trees?" asked Evelyn.

"There weren't any trees here when we parked."

"Oh, Dad, you never pay attention."

"There weren't, were there, Marie?"

"I didn't notice."

"I swear, when I opened the door, I was standing in the blazing sun."

"Are you okay, Glen? Do you want me to drive?"

"No, I'm fine." He closed the back door. "Still," he muttered, "it's weird." They bumped out of the parking lot to the freeway.

Goodbye trees. Goodbye Adam.

"Okay, my turn now, please, Adam."

"I don't know... Are you sure? It does something to you."

"Yes, yes, please, please."

"How can we do it now? We're on the freeway."

"We can open the window. Please, Adam."

Without turning her head their mother called back. "Adam, just let her do it, whatever it is."

"Okay, open the window. Here." He gave her the cone and she shook a few seeds into her hand. "Now breathe."

"I feel dizzy."

"I know. Do you feel yourself moving into the seeds?"

"It's like they're part of me now. Here you go, seeds." She dropped them one by one out the window. "Ooh, it almost hurts."

"They're sprouting!"

The van sped rapidly along but they could see a green haze appear far behind. Soon there were no cars following. "I think we blocked the road."

They laughed happily. "Cool!"

"Let's do it again!"

By the time they reached the city at dusk, they were vegetating in a peaceful stupor, a vast part of themselves strewn along a finger of forest for hundreds of miles through the valley to the park. They leaned against each other drained. Their parents opened the door and helped them out.

"Leave that pine cone in the garage, Adam."

"No, it's a souvenir of our best vacation ever."

"Yes, Mom, it's our magic pine cone."

"You too, Evelyn? Okay, bring it in."

Their father supported them up the steps to the house while their mother unloaded the van. "These kids are as heavy as logs."

"Time to get up," called their mother. "First day of school!" The words came from far away, dimly penetrated the dream of an immense continental forest. Rising from slumber was

like uprooting a small tree. Adam and Evelyn pulled themselves out of bed and went to the kitchen for breakfast. The
morning newspaper reported the bizarre growth of a mixed
deciduous and evergreen forest centered on the southbound
lane of Interstate 5. Trees were spreading east and west despite attempts by road crews with chainsaws and bulldozers
to clear the highway.

"That's terrible!" said Adam.

"That's strange," said their father. "I didn't see any trees."

"It must have happened just after we passed by."

Evelyn and Adam smiled at each other.

"You kids are going to be late. You'd better make like
trees and leave."

They laughed and got their backpacks. Adam put the
cone in his and they went out the door. During show and
tell, when everyone was telling what they had done during
the summer, he took it out and said, "We went camping and
I got this magic cone. It grows trees."

His classmates snickered, and the teacher said, "Yes, Adam,
it is magical the way new life sprouts from a seed."

"No, it isn't like that. You breathe on the seeds and part
of you goes into them and trees grow up right away."

Ms. Hargrave looked concerned and everyone else laughed
out loud. Adam regarded them steadily with the clear gaze
of a spreading forest. "Watch," he said, and shook the cone,
breathed on the seed in his hand, felt faint, stood and walked
to the terrarium on a table in the corner, and dropped it in.
He sat woodenly on the floor and saw the green flash and a
tingle of motion as a tiny stem twisted into a bonsai cedar
that barely peeped above the glass walls.

The classroom was silent. Then his friend Jesse said,
"Wow," and they all crowded around the terrarium. "May I
look at that cone?" asked Ms. Hargrave with her hand out.

Adam backed away. "No, I'd rather not."

"Let me look at it," said Jesse.

"No, no," said Adam. The others pressed close, demand-
ing, and he opened the door to the playground and stepped

outside. His classmates followed.

"Wait!" said Ms. Hargrave. "Come back here!" Some of them hesitated. "Give me that cone, Adam."

"I'm sorry," he said. A crowd stood in the doorway watching as he shook out a handful of seeds and breathed softly, breathed his soul out surrounded by the wavering outlines of the school building and dimming outlines of her friends, inhaled a dream of green life, a wordless song of sylvan speciation, and stumbled and slipped to the ground scattering the seeds.

He became aware again. Evelyn had her arms wrapped around his trunk. She was sobbing and her sorrow distressed him. "Don't cry, Evie," he said and bent his branches to enfold her.

"I was looking out the window and I saw the trees growing up and I knew what you'd done, so I got up to see better and Ms. Hascall said to sit down, but I saw you lying on the ground so I said my brother's hurt and I ran downstairs and you were here and your skin was getting hard and you wouldn't move and I held onto you and you changed, and you changed, and now you're growing here in the yard..."

"Evie," he sighed, and emanated a gentle wave of love which filled her arms and body and flowed through her feet to complete the circuit underground at his roots. "Evie, you must join us. Everyone must join us. Come into the new garden. We need your help, we're still too few—they're cutting us down on Highway 5, you know."

"Yes," she said. "I see," she said, as she saw what he had seen in the grove and now showed her, the completion of the dimly sensed vision of integrated intelligence and interwoven life, individual death and the sparkling green continuum of existence. A crow alit in his branches and laughed with raucous delight. "But what about Mom and Dad? We can't leave them alone. They'd pine for us."

"Tell them to come and join us, or else they'll be left behind."

Adam heard the murmur of an excited crowd of children milling around the trees. The principal stepped forward with Ms. Hargrave. "What's going on, Evelyn? Where's Adam?"

"He's this tree."

Mr. Thierry frowned. "Evelyn, Ms. Hargrave says he disrupted the class and ran out here. We're afraid something's wrong."

Evelyn smiled nervously. "I don't think it's wrong, Mr. Thierry, but I don't think Adam's coming back. Can you call my parents and ask them to come right away?"

"There's the pine cone," said Ms. Hargrave.

Evelyn snatched it up. "Please, Mr. Thierry."

"See if you can get the children back in their classrooms," he said to Ms. Hargrave. "I'll call their parents."

"Come with us," said Ms. Hargrave.

"I'll wait here," said Evelyn.

Mr. Thierry threw up his hands. "Promise not to go anywhere." As they left, Evelyn heard him say, "The first day of school's always tough, but this takes the cake. What are we going to do about these trees? Okay, everybody, back to class."

A peaceful half hour passed in the shade. Sparrows skipped cheerfully through the leaves and chirped at the crow. A squirrel skittered in from somewhere and shyly extended a delicate paw, scampered up Evelyn's arm into Adam's crown and chattered busily from branch to branch. She leaned back and listened to a song of sparkling streams.

"This is all very good, Adam, but I'm not sure one cone is enough to change the whole world."

"That is why, O sister mine, we need the others. Tell them, you who still have their attention, what to do. As these groves quickly grow and fructify, each cone contains the same celestial seeds. Bring the children here and let me speak to them."

At recess a swarm of curious children came. The teachers stood in a group by the building and wondered about the new laurel grove and chatted about the students' strange behavior. The children enthusiastically surrounded Evelyn with questions as she called for calm, eventually settled into a generally attentive huddle, encircled a tree, even the skeptical ones, arms on each other's shoulders, stood silently as if listening intently, then lined up to receive something Evelyn shook from a pine cone, dispersed to the edges of the playground, touched hands to mouths and flung them away. The teachers watched in disbelief as the playground flashed, was covered by a hazy verdant stubble which rose and rapidly veiled the adjacent freeway with a tender growth of laurels as the children skipped laughing and shouting under its canopy.

"I think we'd better start calling all the parents," said Mr. Thierry. "Ring the bell for classes. Let's keep the kids inside. And let's call, let's call... I don't know. I'll call the Park Department." Some of the teachers went inside. The others suggested holding class in the grove; everyone was too overwrought to sit still, and it was a nice day. They gathered their classes and asked what was going on.

"It's Evie! No, it's Adam!" "Where is Adam, anyway?" "He turned into a tree!" "Come on..." "Yes, he did, I saw it." "That's what Evie says." "I felt it, too, I felt like I was a tree." "Me, too! Me, too!"

Their father arrived. "What's going on?"

"Evelyn's sitting out there in that grove and she won't leave a tree she says is Adam."

Glen was astonished. "Where did those trees come from?"

"I don't know," said Mr. Thierry. "Strange things are happening."

"Where is she?" Glen threaded his way through the trees. Evelyn ran and threw herself into his arms.

"Oh, Dad! I'm so glad you're here! Is Mom here, too?"

"Not yet, but she's coming. Where's Adam?"

Evelyn drew him and placed his hand on Adam's bark. Through his palm, up his arm, into his heart came the loving word, "Daddy."

"Adam!" he touched the tree with his other hand, and his mind filled with a bright starlit vision of immensity and a small green globe spinning in serene joy. "Adam, what is this?"

"We're helping to save the world, Dad, and now it's Evie's

turn to join us, but we want you and Mom to come, too. Will you?"

"What does this mean?"

"There is no meaning, Father, only life's dance, and in this place we are the new race of earth being born. If we survive, life will continue here; if not, it will not, and that would be sad, but races like individuals die and creation will continue elsewhere. But life loves living and to live we must evolve, and now we must change quickly. Please come with us."

"Adam... what is this vision? How do you know this?"

"We are the primeval forest, Father, we are Adam and we are the birds, we are the life that lives, the love that loves, the past uncounted, the present extended, the future foreknown."

"Yes... I feel Adam, and I feel the rest of you... But why now, why here?"

"The eternal is always here."

Marie arrived. "What is all this? Hello, Evie, darling. When did they plant these trees? Where's Adam?"

They showed her. "Oh," she said. "Hello, dear." She embraced him and listened. "Yes, of course we'll come. You're our children. We love you."

"Oh, Momma," Evelyn said with joyous relief.

"Show us how."

"Like this." She shook out a seed. "Breathe on it. Plant it." She sighed and sank down.

"Evelyn!" cried Glen. They knelt and took her in their arms. A smile played peacefully on her face, hers eyes closed, the cone dropped. She grew heavy, they laid her carefully on the ground and caressed her thickening skin; she gently kissed her father's hand. "Her bark is worse than her bite," Glen said softly.

"What naughty children; they've gone and left us."

"Well, children always do, you know."

"And now we follow," Marie smiled, and shook the cone, and handed it to him.

By the Skin of His Nose

The wonder of it was that she walked at all. Her smooth transparent body, the visible parts, that is, head and hands and legs, appeared to be hard ceramic-like plastic, the kind that resists abrasion and chemical attack. I trotted along the sidewalk to catch up. The signal at the crosswalk changed, she stopped, and I walked full tilt into her and grabbed her shoulder as if to steady us both and exclaimed, "Oh, excuse me!" Yup, hard as ceramic.

She turned to face me. Eyes, nose, cheekbones and mouth were the mere suggestions you see on mannequins these days. It crossed my mind that this was not a thing you could call female, but since it wore a dress and had a womanly shape I decided to think of it that way. The slight eye concavities were less transparent and their disconcerting translucence distorted the street beyond. She was unquestionably aware of me, since the indentations were directed at my eyes, but without a sign of recognition, the way a camera records your impression without acknowledging your existence.

More than that: The body was clear but these indentations, these 'eyes,' contained something the body lacked. Sometimes in a person with a strong presence you may sense that there's not much soul; their aura is projected by physical solidity and not by thoughts and feelings since they have none. In this case things were inverted. Something deep and confusing was behind the eyes but overall the creature was insubstantial. Her turbid gaze befuddled me. I staggered slightly to regain my balance.

We stared at each other for the time it took the light to change; then she turned and strode across the street. A sudden muscular relaxation made me aware of how tense I had become. I regained my bearings and walked to the office.

This is an age of lies. Events are not so much repressed as they are replaced by versions which support an outcome the marketers want you to think is necessary. The marketing realm is the public realm, and since the public realm has always been the place that creates history, it is now the place of the lie that denies history. Politics and marketing no longer actually produce lies; their 'facts' are produced by the larger lies that form their rhetoric. 'History' comes into being by means of its own ongoing replacement and you begin to doubt your own reactions, especially when everyone else agrees that what happened yesterday happened as it was shown on last night's news. This is not a new technique, though people like Stalin used it more crudely. Of course, Stalin had no need of refinement—he crushed you if he couldn't convince you.

Had the plastic lady been placed there by an advertising firm? If so, why? A marketing test? But she was rather more sinister than the current crop of in-your-face bogeymen that instill anxiety and fear alongside the cute puppy dogs that tell you what to buy to assuage it.

Was she there to accustom people to Virtual Understanding Version 4.0 before its release?

Had she escaped from some development lab down the peninsula? That seemed unlikely, because the people who work in those places are too competent to let it happen.

Or worse: Had the marketing realm expanded to the point that now people's bodies as well as minds were being molded into plastic simulacra?

Worse yet: Was it that I was losing my grip on things?

Later that afternoon my boss's head across the office seemed to be clear plastic. For a closer look I brought him the report I'd been working on. Normally when he turned to me he would have smiled and wiggled his goatee, but the goatee was missing and his face was featureless plastic. It was unsettling.

I'd had a mild headache and clogged sinuses and I was very tired. Maybe that was the problem. Fatigue makes me fuzzy. A good night's sleep or even a short nap dissolves that kind of constriction, but since there was no chance for a nap just then I immersed myself in work and didn't look at him again.

I went to bed early that evening. As I fell asleep my head seemed to be turning into plastic. Not exactly my head, but its contents, everything inside the cranium. Clear plastic, slightly cloudy, with a corrugated surface like my brain's but less bumpy. And not only my head: My body was encased in a thin layer of plastic. When I focused on it I found that it was inside—my core was congealing. The sensation faded below my chest, but only because I couldn't make out much that was farther down. The thought of living with such a monotonous substance at my center was depressing.

Sometimes there is a barrier between me and the world, an invisible skin, like Khayyam's curtain beyond which are those who have gone before and those who will come after, but I've always taken it as a symbol of our apartness from the world, our observing selves' apartness, the part of us that is not of the world. But we are, after all, of the world. Where else would our parts be from? And what is the world but everything we feel and imagine? Well, it may well be more, but what can we know of it beyond what we sense?

The curtain was not there in childhood and is not there in the morning after a good sleep. It thickens as the day goes by. Sometimes I merely notice it and go on. Other times I press against it and seep through into the wider world and become a node of awareness in seamless fabric. But of course you can't survive in a state of pure awareness. You can't accomplish anything. You have to summon yourself into an entity apart from the tides of sensation, an entity that can differentiate impressions so as to work with them. At those times you're an observer bobbing serenely atop the stalk of your neck. Maybe not you, but that's how I am. Consciousness is complicated and ever-shifting and hard to describe.

Most of the time this happens only when I think about it.

This morning the plastic was gone but I felt that a jolt could bring it back, and then I would stretch around it like permeable skin in direct contact with the world. I would be the curtain and the curtain would be a thin deposition around plastic that occupied the space where I had been. All that would be left of me, myself as a person and the face I present to myself, would be this skin. The living core of myself and the barrier between me and the world would swap places. And if I were the skin, I would be bare, receiving unmediated sensations, interacting directly with the outside. But dead plastic would remain at my core. The situation continued repellent.

Then I recalled Jung saying that one's creativity sometimes presents itself as a repellent character, and I suddenly felt cheerful and hopeful and told myself that my repugnance arose from fear of change. Though I didn't like this manifestation of creative surge, if that's what it was, its semblance was not the point; the point was that I was changing and becoming aware of it.

But was this only a trick to make myself feel better? If the change was actually physical, if I was becoming a cyborg or a robot and this was not a psychic manifestation of my unconscious self, then my cheerful hope would be so much wasted energy. Well, what if it were? Was how I felt about this important at all? Which mattered more: Being something or how I felt about it?

If my core was becoming undifferentiated, unchanging and lifeless, then I must simply accept it. Raise no defenses. If that was what I was, then alas, but so be it. I stepped back from concentrating on the plastic core and saw it as a part of me, but there were also other parts. That was cheering.

Instructions were issued. "Go to Market and Sansome and walk north." It seemed that now it was I who was a marketing ploy, a sandwich man advertising something or other. If there had been a chance of me being the last to succumb and becoming the savior of mankind, the possibility had passed. So much for a band of independent rebels in the woods. So much, at least, for my participation in such a band if it existed. I was now a walking billboard.

The first time I saw those electronic billboards that change their display four times a minute, in a taxi from the airport into Frankfurt, I pointed it out to my companions. "Oh, they're everywhere here," one of them said and they resumed their conversation. Now I was Version Two, an ambulating billboard taking the marketer's message along the streets of San Francisco.

But what was the message? Version Two was an attention-getting medium that hadn't been programmed to deliver a message. It was a display screen on a cart rolling along the sidewalk showing nothing but the blue before the signal.

Or was the message more subtle than I thought? Was the medium itself the message? My own reaction when I'd first seen the woman and my boss had been confusion, dismay and anxiety, if not fear. The marketers like to maintain a certain base level of fear that renders everyone more amenable. Hence so many stories about child kidnappings, car hijackings, high unemployment.

There's little more to relate. I took the events to mean that I should find another job and stop thinking about the loss of the public realm. An ad agency liked my proposal to use geckos in a campaign for all-weather tires, which, I am sure, saved the lives of many a cute puppy dog. My new boss was clean-shaven, and finally I forgot about all this.

OBITER DICTA

Which is better: *obiter dicta* or *incidental remarks?*

Obiter dicta evokes elite English schools through the 1930s or so, where Latin and Greek were learnt as a matter of course, and would show that I'm educated in the standard canon, though it might also suggest a certain stodginess and deplorable adherence to the antiquated and slightly racist outlook of a group of privileged gentlemen, not American either. Nor can I recall seeing it used in the last hundred years anyway. No one knows Latin these days, not even Etonians, so there's a high chance of looking priggish.

Worse, I may annoy readers by sending them cursing to the dictionary, although some may find it an opportunity to learn something new, and those are readers like me who am happy to learn a new word, although if there are too many I despise the author for showing off or lacking the common sense to write plainly and in either case demonstrating a certain arrogance.

On the other hand, is it not better to assume a high level of literacy and intelligence among my readers, treat them as I treat myself, respect their capabilities? Shall I give them cause to complain of being underestimated and call me arrogant for prejudging them? And I do deplore impoverishing the language. Shall I dumb my speech down to what I assume is current usage? I might be wrong, anyway.

And yet, is *Obiter Dicta* a proper appellation for the piece? For *obiter dicta* also means a judge's incidental expression of opinion, not essential to a decision and not establishing precedent, and may with its judicial overtone mislead the reader into supposing that I express some ethical judgment.

   Incidental remarks is more neutral but may not be accurate, because some of them are simply curiosities or amusing oddities. It is true that I remarked them—noticed them—but I offer them without comment or remark (considered thought). They are indeed incidental to anything of any real importance, although perhaps notice of the extent to which war and its descriptors enter daily life is not incidental but actually pertinent.
   Some are actually remarks.

INCIDENTAL REMARKS

Contingency and Operational Procurement Exhibition: Title for a torture device convention that took place in London in 1996.

A shop in Grand Junction, Colorado: War Surplus and Louie's Shoe Repair.

Actual Dodge model names:
Avenger, Caliber, Challenger, Magnum, Viper, Nitro, Ram.
Suggestions:
Nuke, Anthrax, Holocaust, Panic, Machismo.

Title for a study: The Politics of Self-Abuse.

Nothing wins against eternity.

Death cures us of our desire for immortality.

In how many languages is 'life' feminine?

Most people take life the way one takes a bus.

A waist is a beautiful thing to mind.

With a little effort, you could have been quite normal.

You're so sexy.
Heck, I'm just trying to keep it up.

Proust points out that absence makes the heart forget and eventually stop craving love's perpetuity.

If you love life like a mistress, will its absence make you eventually stop craving its perpetuity?

A man with a loudspeaker voice, complete with static and interference.

Tips I'd Like to Pass On to my Kids

Knives sharp side down in the drying rack.

Folding money from the bank into the pocket, not the wallet.

In crowds, wallet in front pocket, not back.

You're visible when you walk along a ridge.

Turn pot handles so they don't stick out over the edge of the stove where they can be bumped.

Don't buy a pair of shoes if they chafe at all in the store.

It doesn't matter when ironing shirts if every wrinkle is flattened because as they hang in the closet for a week water vapor in the air will wrinkle them anyway. What matters is to make the creases sharp, since that's what is noticed.

When you turn off the heat under a pan of boiling water, the quantity of steam suddenly increases. Maybe the hot gas rising around the pan convects it away, or maybe the heat increases the air's capacity for vapor and now that the air is cooler, the vapor condenses. I've never known why. If you find out, tell me.

What matters most at work is showing up on time.

Polish your shoes to make a good impression.

If you have a bad feeling about someone in any kind of deal, don't consummate the deal.

Sorry kids, that's not much.

REVISION

v.1   The trouble with my writing is that it gets shorter each time I revise it. I cut away the extraneous words until only the lapidary essential is left.

v.2   A problem with my writing is that each revision shortens it by cutting extraneous words to the lapidary essential.

v.3   Each revision I make by cutting extraneous words shortens my writing.

v.4   As I cut extraneous words, my writing becomes shorter.

v.5   Each revision shortens my writing to the essential.

v.6   I cut to the essential.

v.7   Nothing remains.

v.8

WRITERS WORKSHOP

My imaginary name is [blank] and I chose this name because today I feel [blank]. I would like to write a journal full of [blank], but I'm afraid to because [blank]. The notebook I bought to write in will remain blank. If my journal could talk, it would say [blank] tonight. I hope everybody in this room is [blank]. The person next to me this sentence no verb.

CHRIS'S KETTLE

Chris's café/breakfast bar is hurried this morning because it's crowded and he has some new help. He's running around pouring coffee and returns to the coffee maker with a half-full pot and finds the three warmers each have another pot. He takes one that is almost empty and hastily pours its remains into the pot he's holding so fast that coffee spills onto the counter. He's jerky and looking hassled.

I go to the register for change for a pack of cigarettes and he comes charging over from the coffee. I expect him to be upset at a mere change-making operation but no, he gives me the coins with a warm smile and says, "Thank you."

I think this must be a purely automatic reflex: Be Nice to the Customer. But no, he talks to everyone and takes the time to joke. He is hurried but his interactions with people are not hurried.

I say, "I'm the one who should thank you," and he smiles, nods, and leaves to spread coffee and jokes among the tables.

Morris Comforte

"Things damn well are changing, and not for the better," said Mike. "Morris Comforte could have run this place better." They all laughed.

"Did I ever tell you about being with Taylor when he found out?" asked Alan.

"I haven't heard that story," said Dorothy. "Tell me."

"Taylor came last fall and asked if I was free for an hour or two. 'Sure, what's up?' I said. 'We have to go see Chuck Rivera,' he said, the attorney, you know, and that was all he said. I was a little puzzled. As we drove he said, 'It's about Morris. I guess he signed your name to some papers and Rivera wants you to check the signature.' I asked what kind of papers and he said it had to do with a transfer of funds in Hong Kong."

"The Hong Kong connection," laughed Mike. "The famous Comforte family business."

"I started laughing and said there always something about Mo's stories that didn't hang together, but John looked very unhappy, so I shut up. Then he said, 'It's not like he's a child molester.' He told me some guy loaned Morris six hundred thousand with the Comforte estate as collateral, but now it turns out there's no estate."

"And no money," laughed Olive.

"And no medical degree, and no fish farm, and no Mayo Clinic either," laughed Mike.

"So Taylor's telling me that if you're going to do business, you need to check your partner's background. It's the other guy's fault he lost his money—he shouldn't have loaned it to Mo. I asked him, 'Don't you think what Mo did is criminal?'

He said, get this, he knew a guy who turned out to be a child molester—that's criminal, that's sick, they should've hung the guy. I just shut up. There's no talking to him, that sleazebag. He's got the morals of a cat."

"But Morris was his best friend, wasn't he?" asked Dorothy.

"Morris was always kissing up to him, and he loved it," said Mike. "He thought Mo was the cat's meow."

"Nobody likes her, him, I mean," Olive put in.

"Taylor was crushed. After I told Chuck the signature wasn't mine—it was my name, all right, but not even close to the way I sign it—he started flipping through a thick file. Newspaper articles about Morris Comforte being sentenced to two years for bank fraud, articles about his escape and recapture. Mo's whole past was bogus, and Rivera started chuckling and asked if Taylor had seen the part about him being bisexual. John just kept moaning, 'Morris, Morris, how could you do this?'"

"You're always surprised when people turn out to be different than they seem," said Dorothy.

"Well, for life to go on, you don't have time to question everything."

The building was being evacuated again because of another bomb threat. Harry and Alan went to ask the receptionist what was going on and she played the recorded call. "Watch out. There's a bomb that will explode in twenty minutes."

"You know who that sounds like?"

"Morris Comforte!"

They laughed. She reran it. "Naw. Almost, but not quite."

They drank to Morris Comforte and the unknown bomber.

"Morris Comforte's around," said Harry.

"Oh, yeah? What's he up to?"

"He called my foreman to ask for his camera back."

"Camera?"

"Last year at the jobsite Andy, the foreman, wanted pictures of the formwork, so Morris got a fancy computerized camera out of his car. He said some Hong Kong friends of his exported them, and he offered to sell it. Andy said no thanks, he'd give it back, but he forgot, and then Morris left in a hurry. So yesterday Andy gets a call from Morris, who says he's in an airplane on his way to Seattle, and he wants his camera back. Andy said sure, how do I get it to you? Morris didn't say, so he asked me what to do."

"Hee, hee, fancy that, an airplane. Probably a phone booth in the Tenderloin. What'd you tell him?"

"I told him he should tell Morris to drop by some time and pick it up."

"He probably stole it anyway."

"Did you know Mario Rivoli spent a weekend at a condo in Arizona that Morris loaned him?"

"No! When was that?"

"Just after he started working here."

"The payoff. You know Rivoli got him his job, right?"

"Oh, yes," said Olive. "Mario told me to hire him as trainee."

"Two crooks."

"That's when Steve and I worked together at Presidio Heights. Morris got many phone calls from people who insisted to know where he is and when he'll be in. Once a very big black man came looking for him. When I told Morris, he looked scared and said never tell anybody where he is. I thought it's strange and I don't want to mix up in his personal life, so I told him I just take the message but I won't do anything else."

"Somebody must've been after him."

"Remember how he always talked about his lawyer and how well he knew the FBI?" asked Alan. "One time he was pulling out of the lot as I drove in, and for a joke—I don't know why I thought of it—I told him somebody'd been around to serve him a subpoena. You should've seen the look on his face! He jerked back and said, what?! He looked so distressed I told him I was just kidding."

Jose came by a week later laughing. "Morris is in jail."

"In jail!" said Mike. "What did he do? Rob a bank?"

"No, worse than that. He stole some telephones."

"Telephones!"

"Old Mo has come down in the world."

Harry stepped up. "Where did you hear that?"

"Oh, I have my spies. Look at this." He showed a copy of an arrest warrant for Morris Comforte, alias Reginald Comforte, alias Morris Reggio. "It seems Morris took a crate of cellular telephones from some store. The owner was driving down Mission yesterday and who should he see but Morris. He stopped, got out, Morris saw him and started running so he chased him down the street. They're rolling around on the sidewalk and somebody calls the cops to report a fight. The cops listen to the guy's story, check up on Morris, and arrest him. So he's down at the county jail waiting to make bail."

Harry laughed. "That explains something. Mo called Fred yesterday to call in a loan and Fred asked me if I thought he should pay."

"What did you say?"

"I told him to forget it. Morris was never going to show up around here again."

They grinned. "What a fall for Morris," said Alan. "From bank fraud to petty theft."

"He's just a cheap con man whose game is up," said Jose. "His secrets are all revealed now.

"I'll tell you a story," Olive said. "Paul and I one time want to eat at Chez Panisse but we can't get a reservation. Morris said he's a friend of Alice Waters, he'll call her. So he said it's all arranged, tell them you're from UNC. So Paul told the headwaiter and he said oh yes, Dr Franklin, your office called, come right this way. Paul almost said he isn't Dr Franklin but I poke him in the arm."

Harry laughed. "Morris made reservations for the chancellor and said it was you?"

"Everything he said was phony."

"Nothing about him was what it seemed."

"You never know about people, do you?"

DATABASE

At Halloween one year, my boss Michael Nada assigned me the task of developing a database that would hold all the project information he tracked—cost, square footage, type (lab, classroom, administrative building)—so that he could determine the cost of a proposed project on his own, the better to ferret out the trickery of campus planners asking for Systemwide money.

I talked to the software consultant he'd already selected and agreed on the terms, and then there was the question of which type of contract to use. Eleanor had told me that database development could be considered contracting, which would require a purchase order, but I thought it would be simpler to consider it consulting, which would not. Since I suspected that Michael didn't know the difference, I wrote a memo describing them and said that because the consultant already had a consulting agreement with the Budget Office, I had prepared an amendment to it for the database work. Did he agree?

Three weeks passed with no answer. I told Michael that the consultant was ready to sign. He said he wanted a contractor agreement, not an amendment to a consultant agreement. I asked if he'd like to review my memo with me. He didn't answer but asked me to find out how a similar contract had been handled; he wanted to know which type this should be before he took it up with Ilspach, his boss. I wasn't surprised that he hadn't read my memo, but I was surprised that he apparently hadn't talked to Ilspach about the database. He implied that he was waiting for something else from me but he didn't say what and I couldn't guess. He didn't accept the copies of the memo and amendment I proffered.

The next day he told me he would talk with Nicole about the type of contract. A week later I left a phone message asking if he'd asked her. Christmas came and went and I reminded him again. The next week he told me to talk to Ilspach's administrative assistant Regina; Ilspach had done something like this and she should know how. I reported back that she needed the account and fund numbers, and he needed to get them from Ilspach. Which wasn't the answer he wanted, of course—not only did it not tell him the type of contract he needed, he had been fishing for a hint on how to approach Ilspach with the idea.

I retyped the budget, added other material, and offered it to him for his presentation to Ilspach, but he asked me to keep it all. I showed him where it was in case I wasn't there when he needed it.

Two weeks later the materials were gone, and three days after that they appeared on my chair with a note saying it was okay to proceed but to see him first. He dictated language adding two years of support services to the contract. I called the consultant to ask if the fee would change with the added scope. It wouldn't, so I changed the agreement and told Michael that I'd give it to Regina when she returned from vacation the next day but one.

The next day he asked about it. "Well, as I said yesterday," I said, "I'll give it to Regina when she returns from vacation tomorrow."

So, finally, three months after I'd prepared it, I turned it in. A week later it was ready to sign. It took a week to go to the consultant and back, and two weeks later she emailed Michael and me that the contract was set up.

Michael emailed, "Damn, did that just come thru? That should pretty much screw up the time provisions of the contract again. Jack, how bad is it? You will have to write a letter for my signature transmitting it, and probably authorizing some change in the dates for the earlier items at least. Or suggesting we discuss the implications for schedule." A minute later he came in and said he would send it himself and told me to call the consultant to find out what effect the late start would have. Since Michael's real wish was that everyone be made as anxious as possible, I didn't bother saying the consultant wouldn't care about a month here or there but gave the poor guy a call.

Thus the database got off to a roaring start.

Development continued apace. No step could be taken without his review and approval and at each step he wanted something new. I took care of his requests within hours but his responses to questions took days or weeks. He periodically complained that I wasn't making enough progress.

Once the database began working, he told me to use it to generate the reports he wanted but the damned thing had become so complicated and cumbersome that I quietly used the old spreadsheet until he found out and explicitly forbade it. Doing otherwise would have been admitting a mistake.

Later, when he told me to find a new job, one of the reasons he gave was that I hadn't taken charge of developing the database.

I didn't mention his own tardiness and lack of clarity but said, "You know, Michael, it's not going to do what you want."

He changed the subject. "Personnel has advised me to write a letter about you to the file."

"What will be in it?"

"What we have been discussing."

What had we been discussing? His wanting me to leave? My request for help finding a job in the System? My handling of the database?

When I told him I'd found another job he closed the door and asked who among the campus project managers would be a good replacement.

I wasn't inclined to help and furthermore wouldn't wish him on anyone. "There's no one I can recommend," I said.

He picked up a pen and asked for the names of the ones I'd been dealing with. I listed them, though I didn't see why he couldn't look in his database.

BAD BOSSES

If you've ever had a job you've had a boss who hones dull workaday life to a keen, tormenting edge.

The boss who looks out number one for himself and nuts to everyone else.

The asshole who helps the company screw you. And for what? A promotion for herself? A majority share and a seat on the board, does she think? The blind sucker is being screwed no less than you. —Not that anyone who doesn't put the good of the company above the good of the people who work for it will be appointed boss in the first place.

The boss who won't admit he doesn't know crap about how to do what you do and is afraid someone will find out. He waits and watches for clues and signals and tries to make you feel bad so you won't see how dumb he is. (The staff will lose respect. His boss will fire him.)

The boss so afraid of making a mistake or appearing incompetent that she won't work closely enough with anyone for them to find out. And since other people working together, especially her staff, might conspire to reveal her, any form of cooperation must be nipped in the bud.

Bosses who won't train staff, or who train them incorrectly, or train the entire staff and waste the time of those who already know.

Bosses who don't trust anyone to do it as well as they can. These ones have to see everything before it goes out. Employees can do nothing on their own.

The boss who doesn't trust anyone to keep themselves out of trouble, since that will get the department into it, and consequently him.

Bosses who care only about the problems they themselves face and are unconcerned about the ones their staff are trying to solve.

Bosses who take credit for success and assign blame for failure.

Bosses who see their staff as extensions of themselves, executors of their will. No independent thought or action is needed and none is tolerated. The concept of people as other individuals is missing.

Bosses who change their priorities so often that staff can't finish a task before the next is assigned. Or give contradictory instructions that staff must follow simultaneously.

Bosses whose mind you must read. The arrogant ones can't be troubled with details. The muddled ones haven't thought through what they want. The nervous ones haven't the time to explain themselves because they've jumped on to something else.

The boss who is unclear so she can later deny that that's what she said or what she meant or what she wanted and can berate the employee for not doing the right thing.

Meddling bosses who think things can always be improved. The clients are happy, the scores are fine, ain't nothing broke; but let's just fix it up a little.

Bosses who only know how to deal with a crisis. If things are smooth, they invent one.

Bosses who create a needless sense of urgency. (After all, things take the time they take to get done.)

Mean bosses who like to see people squirm.

The boss who just plain doesn't like you.

Bosses who spoil a person's time off. A cheerful, diligent waitress, always filling in at short notice for others who call in absent, closes the restaurant one night, sleeps through the alarm next morning and is late for once. She opens on time, but her supervisor says they might fire her for tardiness. This is the day before her vacation. For two weeks that worry niggles in the background. She returns and calls for her schedule and is told that she doesn't work there anymore. Now, why couldn't they have told her before the vacation?

Salesmen. Not only do they judge your performance only by what you sell, their need to convince you of one thing or another keeps them from hearing what you say.

Bosses who think that workers malinger. Look, although most people might rather be doing something else, most want to do a good job.

Some professionals who are good at what they do start their own practice. They figure they'll make more money, or they like making decisions, or don't like being told what to do. When word gets out that they do good work, they're offered more than they can do themselves. They can either turn some down at the risk of having fewer clients when times get tough, or hire someone to help—but then they have to manage the help and aren't necessarily as good at that.

Owners who would rather have another dollar than a content, stable workforce. Companies are formed for the profit of their owners, of course, and not for the well-being of their employees, but they can still be quite profitable if the employees are treated well. Maybe even more so if employees care about the place.

Vain bosses who insist on kowtow to their title and position.

Bosses who like throwing their weight around, being in control, telling people what to do.

Troubled bosses who don't like anyone happier than they are, who treat subordinates as they would like to treat their spouses.

I described the crummy boss at a new job to a former one, one of the good ones I did have, and he wrote back, "Jack, boss and bully are redundant."

Maybe these people were beaten as puppies, but that's their problem, not mine. My problem is keeping them off my back so I can do my job.

The Proposal

One of the partners in the main office copied me and Norman, the managing partner of the local office, on his response to a sustainability consultant who said he would put us in touch with a contractor who needed commissioning for a California project. The partner had responded that I was the one to talk to but he was copying Norman as the principal in charge. The consultant forwarded the email to the contractor, and I emailed everyone that I would call the contractor if we hadn't heard from him in a day.

The next afternoon KQ told Norman that he'd called the contractor. Clearly Norman had told KQ this was an opportunity to impress the partners by bringing in some work. I said nothing about having been designated as the one in charge but asked how I could help. KQ said I could write the proposal. The contractor wanted an energy model as well as commissioning. I asked some questions that KQ couldn't answer. I asked when we could call the contractor. Three days later he beckoned to me. "Let's call your contractor friend."

KQ introduced me and sat back to work on his computer. I got the information we needed. The proposal would be due Friday, Monday morning at the latest, as the contractor would be meeting with the owner Tuesday morning to discuss it. It was Wednesday now.

"Do you have everything you need?" KQ asked. "How much is our fee?"

"I'd say $20,000 for the commissioning. The modeling I don't know. We should ask Nico."

"I will take care of the modeling. How long will it take you to write the proposal?"

"Four or five hours."

"So long?"

"It takes time to develop the worksheet." This was an estimate of how many hours each task would take us to do.

"Don't do a worksheet."

"I thought you wanted them."

"Only on big projects."

This one was no smaller than another for which he'd demanded a worksheet.

"Okay, then an hour or two."

"That's better. I don't want to spend much time for such a small fee."

"Can you give me the language for the modeling?"

"I will do that."

The next morning, Thursday, I told him I was done.

"Sweet."

"I'll add the modeling information as soon as you give it to me, and then we can send it out."

No word from him the rest of the day. I left for the weekend, since I had Fridays and Mondays off, and figured he would send me the material when he was ready. When I hadn't heard from him by Monday afternoon and knowing that he never told me what he was doing, I figured he'd added it himself and sent out the proposal.

Tuesday I went directly to a jobsite. He called mid-morning sounding aggrieved and told me he'd sent an email last night and that my proposal wasn't on the network. It turned out he'd been looking under another client's name. I told him the right one and he hung up.

I looked at my emails on my phone. He'd sent this at 10:45 the previous night and expected a response? *"Jack: I found no working draft of the proposal on the network this evening. The client was expected our bid today. If you have a working copy at your home computer, I would ask that you incorporated the following text relative to the energy modeling. Please forward on to Gary as soon as possible."*

That afternoon I emailed to ask if he'd found the proposal, but he didn't answer.

A Fellow at Work

Is JF a windbag or a blowhard?

Blowhards try to influence you; windbags talk to hear their own voice.

Windbags bluster but at bottom are kindly, or at least not malevolent. Blowhards would stab you in the back, and they take being ignored or criticized quite amiss.

Work at the IRS

This morning at eight I told my boss I was quitting if I couldn't be given more interesting work.

What I had done for two days was this: Take paperclip off packet of papers and put it in glass bowl. Put top paper on pile of similar papers at top center of desk. Turn last page over and staple to back of packet. Take a third paper, write three things on it (always the same three things), staple to front of packet. Place packet on pile at top right of desk and start again. Then this work was checked by someone else!

Yesterday I asked how long I had to do this. My boss said that after two weeks I would know the job well enough to do more complicated things. I think I know it pretty well now, I said. No, she said.

Last night I thought about the ladder of success and this morning told her I would be stepping off if I couldn't step up, but she was firm about my need for experience. I said okay, sorry you wasted so much time on me, where are the papers I have to fill out to be able to quit.

While I was filling out the papers, some phoning apparently took place, and I was asked if I would like to talk to someone else about a change. Sure. Then there was a question of getting permission from my department to loan me indefinitely to another. The possible new boss said I should call her back in a couple hours. I said okay, meanwhile did she mind if I checked out a job with the school district I had heard of, in case she did not get permission. It was okay with her.

I left the building, checked out the other job, no dice there, went to a friend's house, chatted with her and a visiting French professor of agro-economics, drank coffee, and called the office. They were wondering where I was. I had *left the building without telling anyone!* (Except the lady who would be taking me into her department.) So things were getting balled up down at the Federal Building. Nuts. The lady didn't know yet if she could take me. My friends and I went downtown to look at architecture. I went home and took a nap. Called the office again. Still nothing.

I was in a weird position, not working, not resigned, in limbo, maybe jobless, wondering when I'd find out so I could call a temporary service for work the next day. Went back to the Fed Bldg and things had become more confusing, though not for me—I knew what was happening—but nobody there could tell each other. I had to tell each one what the other was doing, and they still didn't get it straight. A couple were pretty dumb. Finally I talked to some director of some section and tomorrow would be doing more interesting work (more varied, anyway).

Actually, I was surprised by the largesse they showed. I had expected them to say when I said I simply could not do this work another ten minutes under any circumstances: Well sorry, everybody has to start there. They did say that, of course, and also that the work had to be done, to which I replied that the work I had been doing could be thrown away without causing any problems. And they said other things, about the regular path of ascension which must be followed, and the need for patience, etc, etc. But they waived procedures and got me something else.

Now I have drawn attention to myself and must do well. No problem with that. A lobotomized monkey could do it.

PRESIDIO BUILDING 220
San Francisco, California
Mechanical and Electrical Survey & Analysis
Haravan Consulting Engineers
Primary Author: Jack Oakley, PE

February 13, 2015 DRAFT

1.01   PURPOSE/SCOPE

This report purports to document our survey and analysis of the existing mechanical, electrical, plumbing, fire alarm, and fire protection systems in Building 220 at the Presidio, San Francisco, California.

1.02   EXECUTIVE SUMMARY

Some equipment is old and some is new, and some is in between. We kicked some of it.

A.   Mechanical
        1.   Don't kick equipment without steel-toed boots.
        2.   We recommend replacing the cast iron radiators with new, more efficient radiators with self-contained valve and thermostat controls, as used in France and other advanced regions.
        3.   We recommend installing on-off controls on the boiler so that the building when unoccupied doesn't get as hot and humid as it is now.
        4.   Alternatively, a change in leasing strategy could be considered to take advantage of the building environment with no capital investment. We suggest considering incubation of poultry or use

as a childcare facility for future Presidio neighbors. Either case has the potential added benefit of requiring minimal architectural work, as neither chickens nor children are particularly aware of their surroundings. See, however, paragraph 1.02.E.1 below for a possible constraint.

B. Plumbing
    1. One of the toilets works.
    2. One of the sinks works.
    3. There are no towels in the dispenser.

C. Fire Sprinkler
    1. The entire building will be sprinklered, but it isn't now.

D. Electrical
    1. The existing electrical system is almost entirely new. One distribution panelboard in the boiler room is an older panel of undetermined age which understands the art of makeup and almost fooled us. Fortunately, we are experienced engineers.
    2. Overall the existing system is in good condition and should support base building and typical tenant electrical loading.
    3. Don't stick your finger in electrical outlets. Although this provides a quick check on system operational status, fingers are not well enough calibrated to provide useful information on short circuit grounding capacity.

E. Fire Alarm
    1. The existing fire is alarming and unless extinguished soon may severely limit future potential for occupancy. We recommend advising the Presidio Fire Department of the condition.
    2. Smoke detectors are normally added depending

on tenant coverage requirements, but may be dispensed with if the current conflagration continues.

1.03   BASIS OF STUDY

A.   Field visits were conducted to visually inspect the existing systems. No testing other than a finger probe of a single electrical outlet was performed.

B.   The 8/3/95 National Park Service drawings provided information about building systems. We noted that not all the work indicated in the drawings was completed.

C.   A nice guy from the facilities group provided some information about utilities.

1.04   DESCRIPTION OF BUILDING

The approximately 25,000 square foot building is three stories including a partially unexcavated ground floor. There is an attic and a second floor veranda. There is a roof, and there are some sidewalks, presumably to assist pedestrians in reaching the doors. The building was constructed circa 1939. Unfortunately, time constraints precluded confirmation of this information.

1.05   MECHANICAL SYSTEMS

A.   General
     1.   There have been no generals at the Presidio since it was turned over to the Park Service.

B.   Ventilation
     1.   A new toilet exhaust system was installed in the 1995 renovation. The fan was installed in the attic without spring isolators. Vertical ductwork was installed through the middle of spaces on

the floors below, which is one of the sillier things we've seen in a while. Vertical-type fire dampers were installed horizontally at floor penetrations, which is not so much silly as illegal. We suggest speaking to an attorney.

2. The attic is well ventilated by louvers in mansard-type roof extensions, if you'll pardon our French.

C. Heating

1. A gas fired water heating boiler (Iron Fireman model *xxx*) is supposed to provide heating hot water. We think it does, because the building is hot and humid and we can't imagine how else it got that way. But we can't explain the humidity, since the hot water goes through pipes in radiators and the heat that comes out is dry. Unless there's a leak somewhere and water is coming out with the heat. Or unless this is Miami. We recommend checking the radiators for leaks and a map for location.

2. The burner was converted to gas from oil. The flue is combined with the domestic hot water heater flue at the base of an old chimney, through which it rises to the roof, we believe.

3. Boilers have a service life of from 25 to 35 years. The age of this boiler is unknown. However, we do not recommend replacing it unless it is broken.

4. We recommend that a service contractor inspect the boiler to see if it is broken.

5. We suggest that a seven-day time clock be provided for on-off control of the boiler. We suspect it is on all the time now. That would explain the heat. It would further suggest that the boiler is not broken.

6. Ventilation ducts from the boiler room to the outside were installed in the 1995 renovation but the room is hot, humid, and has the odor of gas. We recommend installing a fan on the discharge duct

to improve ventilation. The fan should be spark-proof so it doesn't ignite the gas.

7. The gas odor probably means the burners are not properly adjusted.

8. As an aside, we note that it is fortunate that the gas odor is not apparent outside the boiler room, as it could kill chickens. We would suggest consulting an animal husbandry expert.

9. A duplex pump (*mfr model xxx*) moves water from the boiler to the distribution system *or vice versa.*

10. Cast iron radiators under windows on the 1st and 2nd floors provide heat. Radiators on the ground floor are suspended from the floor slab above, and there are three unit heaters, in various states of disrepair, consisting of fan and hot water coil.

11. We suggest moving the ceiling radiators to the floor, where they will provide better heat and be less susceptible to seismic activity.

12. We recommend replacing the unit heaters with radiators.

13. We recommend replacing the radiators with a central gas-fired heating system.

14. We recommend replacing the central gas-fired heating system with Franklin stoves.

15. We recommend replacing the Franklin stoves with barbecue pits.

16. We recommend opening an Ethiopian restaurant.

D. Other
1. Careful analysis is needed.

1.06 PLUMBING SYSTEMS

A. Natural Gas
1. A 2" natural gas line enters the ground floor gas vault through a Rockwell No. 4 meter rated at 5,000 cu.ft/hr at 2" w.c. and 2,500 cu.ft/hr at ½"

w.c. *What does this mean, Charley?*

B.   Domestic Water
   1.   A 6" water service was installed in the 1995 renovation. The expansion tank also installed at the service entrance is unsupported. We recommend supporting it.
   2.   The nice guy from the facilities group reports that water pressure is 50 psig at the ground floor, 45 psig at the 1st floor, and 40 psig at the 2nd floor. That makes sense.
   3.   *Charley, did you notice if the piping is galvanized steel or copper?*

C.   Domestic Hot Water
   1.   A gas-fired 100 gallon *[check size]* water heater (Rheem 21X100-1), was installed in the 1995 renovation. The flue is combined with the boiler flue at the base of an old chimney, through which it rises to the roof, we believe. This is the same chimney mentioned above.
   2.   An expansion tank should have been installed on the cold water inlet, downstream of the hot water recirculation connection, but was not. Possibly the tank mentioned above was meant to be here.
   3.   We recommend installing one.

D.   Sewer and Storm Drainage
   1.   There are two floor drains on the 2nd floor balcony. We do not know if they function, as there is evidence of ponding on the balcony, though it may be due to the uneven surface and poor slope to the drains. We recommend unblocking the pipes if they are blocked.
   2.   If there is a storm in the building, drainage may be inadequate. We suggest consulting the National Weather Service.

E. Sump Pump
    1. The new sump pump which was to have been installed in the 1995 renovation was not installed. The existing pump is old and rusted. We recommend replacing it.
    2. We recommend replacing the rusted grill over the sump unless it can be used for a barbecue.

F.   Miscellaneous Observations
    1. The plumbing in the renovated washrooms appears adequate but the flush valve levers are on the narrow side of the stalls. *This doesn't comply, right?*
    2. There is room inside the old chimney that could be used for small pipe, conduit, duct risers, or anything else that fits. For routing, see our credemus above, i.e. what we believe. *Check declension. Or is it conjugation? Charley, do you know? It would be "credo" if it was just one of us speaking. (If it were?) On the other hand, we're a noun of multitude since we're a firm. See what Fowler and maybe Strunck & White say. Says? If we can just say "credo" it will be clearer.*
    3.

1.07   FIRE SPRINKLER SYSTEMS

A.   There is no sprinkler system now, but the 6" water service installed in the 1995 renovation has a blank flange for connection (instead of the 6" valve shown on the drawings).

B.   The nice facilities guy has provided water flow information from three adjacent hydrants whose location has been requested. We recommend that he be considered for a raise, perhaps contingent on reporting the hydrant locations.

C.   It appears that water supply is sufficient without a

booster pump. We concur with the Park Service's intent to install a sprinkler system and regret that one has not already been installed. See 1.02.E.1 above.

1.08   ELECTRICAL SYSTEMS

A.   General
1.   Overall, the existing electrical equipment is quite attractive.
2.   The existing service (600 amperes, 120/208 volts, 3 phase, 4 wire) provides approximately 8.5 watts per square foot overall. After accounting for the base building loads which include the elevator, exhaust fans, fire alarm system and miscellaneous lighting and power items, the remaining capacity for the tenant areas is approximately 6 watts per square foot. This will be adequate for office and childcare center use but tell them not to put fingers in outlets. Poultry farms are another matter.
3.   There is no existing electrical service meter. One was not installed as called for in the 1995 renovation drawings. Like our mechanical colleagues, we recommend contacting an attorney. We understand from the nice facilities man that the Presidio is installing a meter at the transformer that serves this building and that this work is outside the scope of this project. We believe this is appropriate, as our scope of services does not include installation of meters. Furthermore, in America foot-pound dimensions are typically employed. If the Park Service desires use of metric, we will be delighted to provide a separate proposal for additional services. We might mention in passing that we would have appreciated being told about it earlier so we could have included it in our proposal for this survey. The Park Service should be aware that unless the ultimate use of the building

is for poultry, wild goose chases like this cost time and money that could be better allocated.

4. The existing main service entrance switchboard is new and appears in good condition. It does not need makeup and is quite marriageable in its current condition, although we do not recommend delaying solicitation of proposals past its youthful bloom. The electrical room has some water piping in it at the end opposite the end where switchboard is found, near the end. A strict interpretation of the code would require that this piping not be at either end or in the middle either, or the sides. We do not believe this is a problem, though, because the contractor who performed the 1995 renovations seems to have gotten away with quite a bit and the Park Service does not appear to have had an attorney. It is possible that a tenant might, though. Unless one does, we do not recommend relocating this piping unless there is another reason or unless you think it is a good idea, with which we concur.

B.   Power Distribution

1. The existing electrical distribution in the building is new and appears to be in good condition. Adequate branch circuit panels have been provided on each floor. If the tenants opt not to use electricity, no added panels are likely to be needed. The panels may need to be relocated depending on the layout of the tenant spaces, unless, again, the tenants don't take any electricity, and they might not, if they've ever realized how dangerous outlets can be. Or unless they are chickens.

C.Lighting

1. The standard 2' x 4' lighting fixture used throughout *complete this*

2. *We recommend*

D. Emergency Power
    1. Emergency
    2. Emergency
    3. Emergency

1.09 LIFE SAFETY SYSTEMS

A. Good idea.

1.10 CONCLUSION

A. We assume that the fire has been extinguished but are unable to confirm this.

We recommend further study. *Or do we?*

Here's How It Is Now

I'm a very self-unaware guy, very hard-working—when it comes to responsibility, I'm unparalleled—with a spotty sensibility regarding other people—that is, I usually am so focused on my own problems that I don't respond quickly to their moods—though I cry easily at tragedies, happy endings, graduations, marriages, funerals, and Italian operas—and my balance is poor. I'm a good skier but never could stand up on a surfboard though I tried for three years, and I can't stand on one leg.

My wife says I have a heavy spirit, an unenthusiastic presence that dampens everyone else's delight. I am a wet blanket. I wondered aloud the other day why we are living in a rented apartment when many people with lower incomes own houses. She said that because of the decisions I've made, my never-be-in-debt ethic, my work work work don't take a risk attitude, my fantasy of saving enough money to stop working, I've chosen this course myself. Well, I haven't had this good income forever, and until recently we had debts, the repayment of which I thought we were agreed on.

Forty years of work have had an effect. Sometimes I feel ground down. It's true that I chose to have a family and then a second family, and that I also believed a consequence of that choice was the need to have a steady, decent income to support them. Neither of my wives made much money. This one is developing a website she expects to make a lot of money, and our new publishing company has issued its first book, a collection of reminiscences she wrote and I edited. If these enterprises do actually take off, as she swears they will, then I can stop working for a salary and devote my time to them, which will be fun. So I've been inclined to build up savings that will tide us through the transitional period of low income.

But I want to point out that since I met her twelve years ago she's been saying that in another two or three years she'll be making enough money that I can work less or quit altogether. Has she only been saying this to cheer me up? No, I think she has really believed it. It may actually come to pass now because the enterprises she's working on have better practical chances of success than her earlier ideas, and they're actually moving forward.

This is an indication of my heaviness and sober thoughtfulness: Instead of excitement at our prospects I digress immediately into calculations of our income. But how am I to change? A friend consoled me by telling me that she's in a twelve-step program to overcome indebtedness and the attitudes that lead to it. Her mentors tell her that we should have Class A and Class B jobs. Our Class B job pays the rent. In our spare time we work on Class A, and eventually it takes more of our time until we can quit B and devote ourselves to A. An excellent idea, and one which I happen to have consoled myself with for years. My friend says her mentors say it really happens. That's good to hear.

My friend asked why it is that the workplace operates on anxiety and fear. Why are bosses so unpleasant, why do they so demean us, when the institution is bad enough and a little consideration on their parts would improve life for everyone? I said I didn't know if it had to be thus, nor did I know quite how it came to be, but I thought it had to do with a combination of capitalism and democracy; capitalism needing workers, and people not being naturally inclined to work, some sort of coercion is necessary, and in a democracy the coercion must be not obvious but subtle. She agreed. Any thinking person agrees. Many have said this; I'm not particularly perspicacious.

My wife says I've had four jobs since she's known me and I quit each one because I couldn't stand my boss. She agrees that they were all assholes but says it shows that I don't accept the fact that I'll have to continue working for several years; if I did, I would find a way of relaxing and accommodating myself.

I do get quite upset about the way my boss treats me. It eats at me. My wife speaks the truth when she says that I'm always talking about quitting or afraid of being fired. She expects me to snap at any time, and is thankful that at least I haven't broken down on her.

She told me I have unrealistic fantasies about moving to Paris or Istanbul. Maybe so; there are plenty of obstacles including the need for income, difficulty of working as a non-citizen, the effects of a move on our son and his education, our aging parents and their need for care and our need to spend time with them. But she has said she would like to live in France for a couple years, and that Istanbul would be good because it's near Iran without being Iran and is near Europe too. Is it fair to criticize me for having fantasies she has supported?

She said yesterday that she doesn't think we can live in Europe, but we should be able to take long vacations as the publishing grows. Well, this is a fine idea, and it could be a better way than living there to fulfill my desire to spend time there. Then she criticized me for not having talked of it. If she has been thinking this for some time, what kept her from suggesting it? Is it fair to criticize me for not discussing something I haven't thought of?

She said that my family and I are curiously unaware of what we think and feel. Could be. We tend to notice injustice, especially when it comes to how we are treated—in my case, how my bosses treat me—but also what's fair from a societal standpoint, and some of us have modestly acted to rectify a few wrongs: One of my sisters teaches high school, my dad was an environmental activist who brought lawsuits against power companies for obfuscatory environmental impact reports, I write an occasional letter to the editor and have chaired non-profit committees and boards. Not much, truly. My older two kids are labor activists, but she criticizes them for acting out of guilt and not enjoying life enough.

I agree that I should change. I wonder how. Why do I want to? I'll tell you: I want to keep living with my wife. She's bright, she's enthusiastic, and she's kind. I don't want her to leave me out of frustration or boredom. I want her to be happy with me.

She said that my heaviness was apparent the first day we spent together. So I ask why she chose me to live with. She has never answered directly but I think she was of an age when her chances in the marital market were declining, she wanted children, and she took the best offer that came along. She has not denied this, which does not make me feel good. It makes me feel bad.

She does, or did, appreciate my good qualities. Besides helping with the dishes and being a good father and not screwing around with other women (though sometimes I wonder if she would think more of me if I did), I'm a decent poet, a good editor, a percipient interlocutor about politics, literature and music.

I found some solace in her saying that things would change when she begins earning money herself, because rightly or wrongly she hasn't felt that she has a say in the disposition of the money I earn, and when she begins to make her own decisions it will be my decision to stay with her or not. The solace is in her willingness to let me stay. Not particularly cheerful, but maybe I'll change somehow in the meantime so that she'll want me to stay.

She says I don't get along with people. That's not true; I do. My job requires getting along with people, and I'm good at it. But I suppose those are professional relationships that don't go very deep. I feel like the solipsistic character in Joseph Heller's *Something Happened,* where nothing happens until the end. It's a slog, a hard book to read, like Julien Gracq's *Le rivage des Syrtes.* If I am heavy, dull, and slow like that then of course I am hard to get along with.

Here I am with our son at a classmate's birthday party on a lovely day at a park at the Berkeley Marina, and instead of chatting with the parents, I'm being introspective and antisocial writing this down in the parking lot. If I show this to her, will she see that I do think about things, that I do contemplate myself? (She told me I was most interesting during the time we were reading Freud and I told her my free associations.) But these thoughts are pedestrian and not insightful; this merely records what is happening. I'm afraid of showing it to her as it may be more evidence of heaviness.

On the other hand, I can't write like Bolaño. That is, I can write like him, but I can't imagine characters and situations like he does. Clearly, he has taken chances in his life. Or has the imagination to create characters who take chances. I suppose I could create characters who take the chances that I don't. But I'm too heavy, which I say without sarcasm.

And what if Bolaño did take chances? He lived a non-familial life, evidently, though he had a family at the end. Was he a good father? I'm curious. It doesn't matter to appreciation of his work, unless you're a Chinese literary critic. Some say he was a junkie for a while. His wife and mistress deny it and I'm inclined to believe them. Me, I took quite a few drugs in my youth, but I had what I thought was the good sense to stop when I felt the danger of becoming addicted. Did I also stop taking any kind of chance? I think not.

Some major choices have been economic. I could have kept working at shit jobs, Class C jobs, and written and written until I created some work worth reading. Instead I chose a Class B career, went back to school, became an engineer and progressed to decently paid management positions. Frustrated all along in many ways, knowing that I was not realizing my potential to write, I told myself that I was only postponing it. My wife says I should have gone to graduate school and become an academic, which would have been a Class A job for me.

At least I'm not like a woman I once knew whose goal in life was to work at the same job until she could retire with a good pension. She liked me because I was arty; unlike her husband I liked the opera, and I read poetry to her, though she too didn't quite approve of my changing jobs when I got bored or reached my limit of boss toleration.

Back at the birthday party are mothers with highlighted hair and fathers in running shoes and t-shirts advertising progressive causes. Affluent white middle-class folks with a store-bought decorated birthday cake. This being Berkeley, we are surrounded by African-Americans, Latinos, Russians, Indians, Muslim women in hejab, good-looking young men discussing restaurants in European accents. The birthday party is made up of ordinary people with nothing new to say. But is this any worse than spending the night after a prize fight drinking and snorting cocaine with a few Mexicans and prostitutes in Ciudad Juarez, blow job in the back yard, uppercut to the jaw of a guy holding a pistol in the bedroom, like a Bolaño character? Though a good drunk or a fuck with a stranger is fun, as a lifestyle it is no more interesting, at bottom, than discussing project management with a San Francisco condominium developer.

I told a guy at the party about my wife's complaints about my heaviness. He was surprised; he thought that being a good provider and a good father is what women look for. That's why his eighteen-year-younger girlfriend chose him. I think he's right in general, but my wife aims higher than a dependable provider. Sometimes I wonder what she would do if somebody like Bolaño appeared on the scene.

It occurs to me that her forgoing to act according to her wishes resembles mine. Has she changed because of me? Is she using my traits as an excuse for not acting as she would like? Is she upset with me or with herself? Do these traits remind her of what she detests in her brother? For thirty years he has had excuses for not doing what he wants to do. He designs cars in the basement of his parent's house—their pensions have supported him for many years, and after his father died he continues, at the age of fifty-six, to live with his mother—but only twice in the eleven years I've known him has he actually shown his designs to anyone who might be interested professionally. He's afraid they'll be stolen, and he declines to show them to idiots who won't appreciate them, and everyone in the automobile industry is an idiot. I think he's afraid they'll be rejected, which they were one time and the other they were ignored.

Their mother just had back surgery and he is medicating himself with steroids, which drastically exacerbates his normal bipolarity. My wife had to tell him to leave our apartment, where he had been staying so he could visit their mother in the hospital. Their aunt arrived from Iran and is with us for a few days until my mother-in-law returns home. All this causes a lot of work for my wife and her patience is shorter.

Do I have the luxury of self-reflection and self-analysis? Her brother has nothing but time and look what he's done with it. He's freer in spirit than I am, yes, like my wife, like their parents. They've all done as they liked with their time and their activities. It's true that I haven't their flexibility of spirit, which may have come from their sense of privilege; they held influential positions in Iran before the revolution. Though they had to adjust their lives to live within lessened means, they've always had some (unearned) income they could rely on. Me, I'm weighted by the fear of giving up my income. For the time being I don't see a source except working for pay.

As I see it, when the publishing brings in money, then I can work less, or I can work less when Social Security becomes available at sixty-two or sixty-five depending on how much income I want, or we can move somewhere where living is cheaper. But I do owe our son a childhood free of want and a college education, so my considerations must include that. As for her wants, what does she want? Is it a house she wants? She keeps saying they're overpriced and wants to wait until prices drop. I agree about prices but I don't care and I'm willing to buy now, but she says no. I'm happy to let her decide, but this irritates her; she says it's an example of my apathy.

Seems like the only thing I can do is write more, about what I know, and try to find some meaning in it, and if there is none, which seems more and more likely—apart from the meaning that comes out of drawing connections between things—try to give a sense of time and eeriness and timelessness, which makes you feel for a moment that there is something bigger than you that you can tap into, or wish there were, or at least feel that there are other people who feel the same way you do.

JAMES WALKER

(Homage to Roberto Bolaño)

James Walker (1970–2023) American, b. San Francisco, CA, d. Whitefish, MT

After several youthful poems—angry exposures of social injustice or impressionistic barings of turbulent emotion—Walker wrote little for the next few years but mortgage loan applications for a company that failed during the 2008-2009 crash. With the proceeds of his personal speculations, he retired to a cabin in the Montana hills and self-published his first collection of mature poetry, *The Poet of the Probable.*

Two hundred copies were sold at the Kalispell sandwich shop due to readings at fraternal organization dinners. Small businessmen with a craving for recognition took a fancy to his recipes for making lemonade from lemons and fruit salad from incomparable apples and oranges. Apples were a local crop and the oranges added an exotic touch, and everyone had at one time or another owned a vehicle with mechanical troubles that couldn't be fixed.

Alone in his valley, Walker found his ideas slowly regressing from the cramped Confucian habits of business piety to the hopeful positivism of his college days. *The Poet of the Possible,* his next collection, explored the yearnings of a mind anxious to reach its natural extents. These poems appealed to a few local hunters and fishermen upset with restraints on free access to private woods and streams, but they were too iconoclastic for his earlier public. Appearances at paintball events sold only sixty copies.

His last work, *The Poet of the Impossible,* reanimated child-hood dreams of magic and infinity. Jungian individuation appealed little to the public, though, and by now he was viewed as an eccentric hermit spouting whatever nonsense crossed his pot-saturated brain. Walker could give away only twenty copies and leave the rest on consignment at the sandwich shop.

Two weeks after his death in a drunken collision that also killed the other family, a spiritualist on his way through town picked up the book for distraction during dinner and found in its anacoluthic structure and bizarre imagery an accurate depiction of Lemurian psychology. He took the copy with him to Mt. Shasta, where one warm afternoon he read selections to a circle of naked people high on the mountain.

BULLSHIT

There's a lot of bullshit around, folks.

There was bullshit on the mountain when Moses came down with the tablets. There was bullshit in Delphi. There was bullshit in Rome and still is. We've got bullshit in Washington, horseshit in Cheyenne, and yakshit in Tibet. Look anywhere you want, any time, and you'll see half the people perched on dungheaps spewing bullshit from their mouths and the other half kneeling before them with mouths open eating it straight. It's one straight flow of shit.

If you all will step up, we are going to examine this flow of shit. We are going to do it backwards, by orifice. We will start with verbal diarrhea, move through a couple stomachs, pass by way of the colon, and wind up at the bull's ass, the source of pure shit.

See all these people running around like their heads are cut off? They aren't cut off, not really. You just can't see the heads for the shit. These people are pouring out the shit they've spent their lives learning. This shit has been around for so long it's stale. You can smell it. It smells like two-car garages, like your boss saying you can't use the company telephone for personal calls. It glistens in the pores of the clerks who head for a pay phone at coffee break. Robert Frost and Norman Rockwell reek of it. So do border guards.

Listen to somebody who knows it when he sees it. He pronounces it boolshit. He says boolshit and walks out and gets another job. "Too much boolshit around here," he says. "What is this boolshit," he says.

Then there's the guy who feeds you boolshit and knows he's doing it. Like preachers, you know, or communists or salesmen. They're feeding you the same old shit but they're doing it for their own reasons. This is called bull*shit*. There is self-interest involved. Somebody tells you the end justifies the means, he's full of bull*shit*. Fellow tells you you need a car to get a date with a lady, this is probably bull*shit*, especially if he sells cars.

That man who quit that bool*shit* job, he probably does a lot of bull*shit*ting. He does it for fun. People are comical when they eat it. When you meet this type of guy, all you have to say is "Bull*shit!*" and he knows right away that you're on to him. The two of you will get along fine and you can run around bull*shit*ting together. It's a gas.

But be careful when you call out bull*shit*. A lot of those preacher types aren't in it for the fun of it; they're in it for the income. You've got to be subtle, feel your man out.

Then there's sheeit. A friend of yours comes up and says he just received knowledge from an old perfect master. This is the same old bullshit, all right, but more refined. It's essence of bullshit. It wraps up the whole shebang and hands it to you in a neat parcel with ribbons on. BUT THE PARCEL CONTAINS ONLY THE SAME OLD SHIT. All you can say to your friend is, "Sheeit, man, what's got into you?"

Take this parcel business. Without losing the scent of what's inside, take a quick look around you. We're in the colon. This is where turds are made. Consider these: mathematics, physics, nation, money, Billy Graham, Krishnamurti, women's lib, macho, nuclear detente, the dialectic, heaven, hell, your birth, your death.

We are standing in a pucker at the asshole. We are now watching Pure Shit pass by.

Pure Shit

is the source, the mother/father lode, the shit lode whence floweth all the others: bull, bool, horse, yak. Pure shit, baby, is something else again.

So far this has been easy. Everyone is acquainted with

various forms of shit. Everyone has a sense of smell. Not everyone can smell it everywhere, because it is everywhere and the nose gets overused and dulled.

So far it has been easy to say this is this kind of shit, that is that kind of shit. But what is it that makes shit shit?

Now that we are at the asshole we can ask what, then, is

Pure Shit

Pure Shit

comes out the hole between the sides of the asshole. It springs from the hole at the center. The sides meet at the center but they are not the center. Obviously. When something wants to come out, it has to pass by way of the asshole, between those sides, which are the symbols, from the simple phoneme to the great religious world-views, that shape Pure Shit. Before it gets there, it is nothing. It is Pure. The Shit comes when it passes the asshole. The asshole is there, shall we say, to pass on purity but all it produces is shit.

I assume everyone grasps what I mean.

A philosopher put this way: He who speaks does not know; he who knows does not speak. In other words, he who speaks is speaking through his asshole.

All the great and little systems as well as the people you meet on the street are trying to catch the purity at the center by crowding closer and closer to it. They are like the parabola which approaches its asymptote but never arrives. How can they? They are mere flesh, and the center is less even than air. As they approach the center they define it, but they cannot become it.

Example: You are in love. You tell your lover, I love you. You have just dropped a turd. Here's why: Your love is in the center of the asshole. You know it's there; you know you're in it. You are in love. Right. Now try to tell somebody else what you feel. *I'm in love.* Do you think that did it? Did you convey the overwhelming expansion of your soul, the blurring of the edges between you and the world and your lover? Did you measure the depth of your heart and the prairies of its breadth? My friend, that was a meager turd you shat.

It would be an unusual lover who replied to *I love you* with *bullshit*. But we do want knowledge and honesty, we want to live in the purity at the center of the asshole. We want to know both purity and bullshit.

All systems and theories hunt purity by encircling it. They squeeze in closer. They eventually get cramped. They frustrate you because you always think you've almost got it. They're full of shit.

If you want purity, you've got to give it room. How are you going to enjoy it if you can't breathe? We need to clear away some of the shit, get some elbow room.

Techniques for Refining the Sense of Smell
as well as
Laughter as a Means to a Happy, Creative Life

God Speaks should be called God Farts.
The old perfect master should develop a stomach ulcer.
The president should get the clap.
The guy where I work, the one who thinks Robert Frost is the greatest poet—because of the bullshit he's read in Reader's Digest—should go to Egypt, his favorite country, and slip in one of the latrines and land with his face down in the filth.
Everything false needs its nose rubbed in its own shit.

You can respond to any question or line of thought in any situation by referring to the Principle of Pure Equivocation.

Equivocation means "all voices are equal." Each symbol is equally incapable of conveying that for which it stands, simply because it is not that for which it stands. You can never say what you mean.

But: You can say anything you want about it.

If you really are set on conveying an idea, you will have to use as many symbols for it as you can come up with. You must present it from different angles, in different words, with many analogies. If you show enough sides and if your listener is attentive, he may get an idea of what you're trying to say.

If you are asked a meaningless question, one that is founded in equivocation itself, that is, in bullshit, in the gap between myth and reality, you can reply only by equivocating. Pop out any random statement. It will make as much sense as anything else.

"Je suis l'âme errante," said Nadja to André Breton when he asked her who she was.

This can be a fun game. You control all possible answers to all possible questions. Pick and choose the answer that most suits your mood. You will have lots of fun if you memorize aphorisms, since they are ready-made equivocations. The work has been done for you. Each aphorism already has associations built in. You won't have to explain yourself at all. You can relax and watch your interlocutor turn blue as he tries to see how your answer replies to his question.

You can also do this to yourself. Suppose that as you are walking down the street in an ordinary mood you are seized with sudden horror: What am I doing here? Where am I? What is going on around me? WHAT HAVE I TO DO WITH ANY OF THIS? These are unsettling questions. Answer immediately: A stitch in time saves nine. Note that it does not answer your questions; it has nothing to do with them. It is absurd.

Don't feel bad. Sit down immediately. This is therapeutic. Compare your questions and your response. Maybe you don't like that response; make up another. Try these others and watch what happens: I am on my way from my home to my job. Or, I am twenty-three years old and I have been to college and graduated; now I am working so I won't starve. That's better. You think you're onto something. But look up suddenly and shake your head violently to clear out the words. You'll realize you haven't answered your questions at all. You're still puzzled. In fact, you're still horrified.

Try again: A stitch in time saves nine. Consider carefully.

Does that tell you any less than your other answers? DOES IT MITIGATE YOUR HORROR? If not, try this one: I am a manifestation of humanity's collective unconscious; I walk and talk and think these thoughts because I was born this way. Or maybe you like this better: I am the product of my times. I am afflicted with the mal de siècle. This is a time of great change and disorientation. Of course I don't know what I'm doing. Nobody does.

A stitch in time saves nine.

If you accept any of these answers, if any of them soothes your horror, go back and reread the first part of this essay. Read it until you can apply it to each to each answer you've given yourself and each is seen to be empty. You'll see that you are full of shit. Now you'll really be horrified. Here you are, standing in horror at your own existence, and all you can come up with is a bunch of shit.

A stitch in time saves nine.

That has absolutely nothing to do with your questions or your horror of existence. NEITHER DOES ANY OF THE OTHER SHIT YOU'VE BEEN HANDING YOURSELF.

Only a crazy man would hand himself platitudes to cure the sickness in his soul. But look, nothing you can say will fill any gap you feel, will build any link from you to what you see. No question you can ask will touch the reality of your situation. Questions are as meaningless as answers.

Examples of Meaningless Questions

What is reality?
Why? (Concerning the meaning of existence)
Who am I?
What am I doing?
What am I supposed to be doing?
Is mankind basically good or evil?
Which came first, the chicken or the egg?
Where will it all end?

The process is purifying. When you see the equal meaninglessness of words, you see the equality of all words.

When you see the equal meaninglessness of the concepts which words express, you see the equality of all concepts.

Concepts are abstract relationships among things. When you see that all concepts are equal, you see that all things are equal.

The Joke

Everything is in your attitude.

Anything can be good; anything can seem bad. It all seems serious.

Here's the joke: You are going to die.

But here's what's serious: You're going to have to live through the rest of your life first. As long as you are alive, you're going to be doing things and you've got to be serious about what you do. If you aren't, it will all be half-assed.

You've got to be serious to get to the center of the asshole. It is hard work cutting away the bullshit, but if you don't, everything you do and say and think and feel will be part bullshit. Not being at the center of the asshole, you will only be half-assed. You might as well be dead.

We need full-assed people. We want people who know how serious life is so they'll get to the heart of the matter at hand and come up with some pure responses. We want honesty. GET SERIOUS.

Want to know what is at the center of your asshole?

It is YOUR OWN DEATH.

When all the bullshit is gone, what do you have left? Your life, sure, but we all know that saying that says nothing. We know too that there's nothing you can say about your life that will make any sense. So ignore it.

There is something that is even more pure than your life, a fact that is more true and absolute than any other fact: It is your death. You are going to die.

When you die, everything that you thought was serious will die with you. All your hopes, your plans, your anguish, joys, hunger, plenitude, all of it is going to croak with you.

Ain't this funny?

It all fades away in a pffft.

Imagine this (or don't image, go back and read the newspapers): The astronauts took a lot of equipment when they went to the moon. They didn't go often so they took as much as they could. They took delicate and unique equipment. On one of the first journeys they made, they had along a piece of equipment that cost two million dollars (in those days!). They set it up along with rest and then one of the astronauts, backing up to take a picture of the other, tripped over a guy wire. It wrecked the equipment. "Oh, gee," said the astronaut. "I'm really sorry, Houston."

Just think of it. All that time and energy from so many people to get that equipment up there. Almost a once in a lifetime chance. You can bet the scientists who had their tests depending on it felt pretty bad. All this, two hundred forty thousand miles through space, and some klutz stumbles on it and breaks it.

You think that's funny. Just wait until you croak. It'll be even goofier.

Your death makes everything you do ridiculous. Everything you take seriously is ridiculous in the face of your death.

This is the point.

Life is serious when you look at it from the standpoint of being alive. Life is ridiculous when you look at it from the standpoint of being dead.

If things get too heavy, pretend you're dead. You will laugh. If things are hectic and ridiculous, start taking some of them more seriously. Arbitrarily pick one thing and work at it. You won't laugh so much.

Become a master of shifting your viewpoint and you will prevail in all situations. You'll also be the odd man out, but which do you want, success or sanity?

If everybody's serious they're going to bring you down. Laugh at them. Laugh at yourself if you're being too serious.

If everybody's being flip, that'll bring you down too, because everything will seem flip and worthless. Remember that life is serious.

We are talking about serious laughter. We are not talking about being flip or smug.

Become a master of shifting your viewpoint. You'll mystify your friends, and even better, you'll mystify yourself.

Another good exercise is putting yourself in somebody else's place. This gives you a new viewpoint on everything, including yourself.

Another one is to put yourself in your own place at some time in the past. You get a sense of personal history this way, and you understand yourself better. Some places you've been are better than others; you can select the best ones and enhance your present attitudes with them.

Some situations shift your viewpoint for you. These are the best, the ones it is worth looking for. Love is one. Service to other people is another. Travel, especially foreign, is another. You might know of others.

A train wreck will shift your viewpoint for you. I myself became enlightened in a train wreck. Of course, you have to live through it to get much good out of it. The wreck was in a foreign country where I didn't speak the language very well. I didn't know what I was doing there. I had no meaning in my life, no passions. I had been feeling lousy all the way up to the wreck.

When the train lurched, I didn't do anything. When it lurched again, the final and definitive lurch which broke my nose on the seat in front, I was miffed with myself as well as feeling lousy because I knew I'd had time to block the blow.

So the instant before the wreck I felt bad, lousy, depressed, lost, lonely, and angry with myself. The instant after, I felt my nose to make sure it was broken and then I passed out.

When I could start thinking again, I realized something wonderful had happened to me. I felt sick, lost, lonely, depressed, and angry with myself, but I was giggling because none of it mattered. I had just lived through a train wreck. I HAD NOT DIED.

I had not died but I might have. From the standpoint of my death, everything I'd been feeling bad about was funny.

Now look: This won't cure all your problems. In fact, nothing at all will change except your outlook. You simply won't care as much.

But the world would change if everyone took themselves less seriously. It's good to laugh at how ridiculous you look.

Well, well, if I thought this would change the world I might get serious about it. As things stand, it's ridiculous to try to change things. I laugh at myself for bothering to write this down. But I did bother, so as you can see I am serious.

But then, this is all bullshit.

Note 1:   Horseshit is a worthy topic but strictly speaking is outside our purview, as it lacks the intent to deceive. It springs from simple stupidity and consists of uninformed blather, the nonsense that people spout when they have nothing to say but are determined to say something. It's not false; it's merely ridiculous and merits no more than an incredulous stare.

Note 2:   Yakshit is a joke.

ABDUCTION ALERT is posted on the freeway signs.
GREY CHRYSLER SUV LIC 1ABC234.

First of all, be afraid. Your child too might be abducted.
What does that mean, abducted? Kidnapped? A stranger in
a car with dark tinted windows rolls to a stop beside your
seven year old daughter on her way home from school...
Wait. Does your seven year old daughter actually walk home
from school? Don't you pick her up? You don't trust people
enough to actually let your kid walk to and from school, do
you? Well, maybe you live in a small town where you know
everybody and they know your children and watch over them
like the sparrows in the field each morning and afternoon,
(but if you do, what are you doing on a Southern California
freeway reading signs?), so it is a real shock, a horror beyond
imagining, when hands reach from the rear door and one covers your daughter's mouth so she can't scream and the other
drags her by the neck into the car, the door closes and the car
smoothly accelerates down main street and onto the road out
of town; but your neighbors the birdwatchers have fortunately
noted the license number and make, model, and color, so after only a mild hassle convincing the highway patrol that yes
there has indeed been a kidnapping, or abduction, as trained
officers of the law and experts in terrorism call it, the information is flashed statewide on the state's freeway signs, even
regionwide, we don't know, we could call the highway patrol
to ask how far the net is spread but don't feel like concocting
a story about writing a newspaper article so they won't put
a trace on our phone to determine if we're a security breach.

But the sign doesn't say KIDNAPPING, does it. Those

are rare. It says ABDUCTION. Some distraught or pissed-off spouse picked up the kid for an afternoon and didn't return him, and the offended spouse called the cops and they don't have anything better to put up on the signs, and it helps deliver the message: Be Scared. Your kids too can be kidnapped any time. Shut up, obey the cops, and you'll be safe.

The End of the War on Terrorism

(The War is Dead, Long Live the War!)

We are SO happy to announce that the Cold War is not over after all! The bad guys are still the Russians!

Whew! It was a rough patch there, the breakup of the USSR, then the nice-guy premiers they had, old pal Gorbie, Yeltsin drunk but friendly, the oligarchs, it looked like the Russkies were just homeys with a heavy accent. What were we gonna do? Do you remember back twelve years, twenty, what was it? The fall of the Berlin Wall! Détente! Friendship! Mir! Drüg! Hoo boy, what was going to happen to all those unneeded defense dollars? Remember? Nobody knew, the talking heads, Ted Kennedy, the Repubs. For a while there Ronnie Reagan had a Star Wars thing going but then he went to Reykjavik and almost called off the arms race! That's how close it was. People were thinking we might have to fight AIDS in Africa or have single-payer healthcare. Remember Hillary during Clinton's first year? Hegemony was gonna have to come through non-violent means like NAFTA. George W Bush was elected and there was antiglobalization, Seattle, lowest presidential ratings since Howard Taft. Desperate times.

And then 911, which was a lifesaver for George and the gang. The War on Terror! The Patriot Act! Osama bin Laden! The Military Commissions Act! Islamic Fundamentalism! Even, for god's sake, Peak Oil and Global Warming!

But mainly The War on Terror. The Endless War, like a Beach Boys song or Annette Funicello movie or Warren Miller ski flick. Chase that bad boy Osama into the hinterlands of Afghanistan, into the North-West Frontier of Pakistan. And anthrax, remember? And the USS Cole. And Saddam, the yellowcake terrorist of Iraq, the pal of Osama, he invaded Iran on our behalf but later went bad, manufactured weapons of mass destruction or something.

It never quite took, though. Much as we tried to get enthusiastic about terrorism, it was always a little forced. Remember Freedom Fries? The Dixie Chicks? All those newscasters stumbling over strange middle-eastern names. Talk shows with university experts explaining the difference between Shias and Sunnis. The history of the Muslim Brotherhood. We tried so hard to learn why it all made a difference.

And Israel grew from our one democratic friend in the region—heck, the region grew into The Region—she moved into the executive branch and became our main partner in the War on Terror, our best collaborator. (Better than any of the EU countries, certainly—remember the French, who wanted conditions, the Spanish pulling their troops out?) Now we softies understood terrorism too, we felt the pain of direct assault, the intransigent Muslim mind, we'd had a lesson, we began to appreciate why we'd been sending so much money to so few for so long, though I must say from personal experience that it still wasn't so easy for a taxpayer from their primary means of support to enter on foot from Jordan—the Friendly border guards must have thought our training needed reinforcement, we didn't appreciate the dangers of standing in the passport control line for the Arabs...

Lessons, lessons, it was so much *work* that War on Terrorism, trying to understand why Musharraf had to go when until now he'd been our staunch supporter in his own Region, and poor Benazir Bhutto—Bhutto who?—not that Small Gods Must Be Crazy author? Oof. We'd had practice in Latin America, but it was so hard to learn a new set of friends and enemies and arguments. We tried.

But now! Calloo callay! The Russians are back. You can see the relief on the newscasters' faces! You can hear the joy in the BBC radio voices! These are the enemies we grew up with! We can say their names! Maybe not the way they say them—that doesn't matter—but the way we say them. We know who we're talking about again. Not those damn Arabic foreigners! The ones we grew up hating when we were kids!

Remember how we used to crawl under the desks for atomic bomb drills? Weren't we cute? It was the Russians! And now they're back! The SOBs invaded Georgia. (Not the one next to Florida, the one next to our Regional Friend.) The SOBs! They're not good guys after all! They're still SOBs! Ah, how warm and fuzzy defending the world's democracies from Communism again.

The War on Terror is over! The Cold War is back! La guerre est morte, vive la guerre!

THE FLAG

A guy at the swimming pool the other day was wearing American flag swim trunks. A big guy, heavy, with shaved balding head, bulked up shoulders and chest, paunch hanging over the waist of the old red, white and blue. He played with his two year old daughter like a good father but looked like he would disapprove if long-haired hippies set fire to their brassieres in front of a college administration building or a non-student foreigner crashed the UCLA library.

Now, I'd had the impression that you need special dispensation from the Directorate of the Flag to use one as anything but a banner flown free and proud. That was the case when I was a kid, but maybe not anymore: you see flag motifs on all kinds of products. I'm too lazy to look up the rules, though— I'm not a fact-checker, just a guy with opinions.

When I was in grade school each day began, "I pledge allegiance to the flag of the United States of America, and to the republic for which it stands: one nation under God, indivisible, with liberty and justice for all." They don't do that anymore, at least where I live, thanks to a couple lawsuits having to do with God. Just as well. What does it mean, pledging allegiance to a flag? Allegiance to a republic is one thing, but a piece of colored cloth?

These days the only place you pledge allegiance is at sports events. In high school I never could put much emotion into a couple square feet of cloth or the games either, or pep rallies, or college or professional sports, especially professional. Sports are just fine, and team sports are great if you actually play them, play together with attention, cooperation, passing, blocking, supporting each other, all that, and when you play together you develop skills that come in handy later in life, and if you're already a working stiff where productivity counts maybe you're benefitting from all that teamwork, and if you're old maybe you've found that it didn't come in handy after all but still you had some fun playing around.

And it's a pleasure to watch accomplished athletes, dancers, musicians, and you appreciate it even more if you've tried to do it. But what do commercial sports have in common with the ones you actually play, or played? It's not you running around the field in colorful clothing, nor is it anyone you know. It's a bunch of salarymen you don't know who work for rich investors you don't know who live in parts of town you don't even know how to get to.

What is there to get excited about? The skills and teamwork and sheer beauty of the thing? Maybe—I hear people use those words the next day—but that doesn't seem to be as exciting as winning. That is, their team winning (not them, because they didn't actually play), and the win seems to be less important than what leads up to it—the win is only the resolution, the sudden relaxation, the release of the tension it took to get there. And despite hand-wrung regrets about violent injuries and the need for a return to gentleman-like contests, it seems that the more aggressive the contest, the more excitement the crowd feels. The whole show is hyped up. Without provocation and violence how could anyone get excited?

Manufacturing is a well-developed business here in the US. And products demand markets, so markets are manufactured. How? By marketing. Marketing is a well-developed business, too. "I am the decider," said President W (which undoubtedly reassured many since, as Hannah Arendt pointed out, people in a totalitarian society—not that the US is a totalitarian society—are relieved when their leader takes responsibility for the awful things he makes them do). But he could have said with equal validity, "I am the marketer." Around here marketing and deciding are done by someone else. But we buy into it, and not only that, we pledge allegiance to it, or the flag which stands for it.

Stupid as pride in a team or a nation may be, it gives one a sense of belonging. You're part of a group, you're not alone in this damned life of commercial isolation. You can bet with your colleagues in another city and chortle when their football team loses (you're the best!) or chin up with a grin and pay up to show you're a good sport when yours loses. It's all in fun. It builds team spirit between the offices. And it's nice to have your World Cup team beat the others, especially when the world is down on you.

Part of the flag fetish of my childhood years was a strong sense of prophylaxis: keep it clean, don't drop it, fold it properly, don't fly it in the dark or rain, don't demean it by wearing it. But things change, and since commerce is actually the main business in America, eventually our right to make money overcame our quibbles. There might still be people who would keep the colors from being dragged through the dirt of commerce, but they're silly. The flag is the colors of commerce.

The guy in the swim trunks surely felt no sense of desecration. On the contrary, he was proud to show his allegiance. And the rest of us were proud to have such pride in our midst. And if there do happen to still be laws about not demeaning the flag by draping it around the wet paunch of a skinhead, we Law and Order folks recognize that some laws must be applied selectively.

Though sometimes it seems like the flag can be a tool for intimidation. A group of picnickers in the park fly one at their table. Don't tread on me or my loud, drunken behavior. A facilities manager I knew displayed a flag beneath his email signature. It probably seemed like a good diversion from the embezzling he was later fired for. My parents put a flag sticker on their bumper as protective colorationin the military town where they lived. Of course, this all happened in the early days of the Bush administrations when the marketers were ginning up support for the War on Terror and the other ones. Now that we've gotten used to its endlessness, you see fewer flags.

That facilities manager's boss was a retired officer who grew up in Brooklyn with immigrant parents, worked hard in school, joined the army, trained at SOTA, was eventually commissioned and spent several years in Central America doing what he once called crowd control and which I never cared to find out more about. He was good to work for—he told people what he wanted and then let them do it. His managers at the three colleges raised the flag in the morning and took it down and folded it properly in the evening, and if he happened to be around he would salute and then stand easy for the ceremony. He took a keen interest in the relocation of the flagpole for a project of mine at one of the campuses. My job was to get things built, not give my opinion about what I was building, so I simply took care of it.

I once picked grapes for a man who owned a small vineyard in France. While we worked he told stories about neighbors in the community and countryside, and who had lived there when he was a child and when his great-grandparents lived and four hundred years before that, and life during the German occupation, and how to hunt rabbits with a ferret, and on and on. Later his son convinced him to write down the stories, and then he died, and afterwards I published them as a book.

The mayor of the town where they lived organized a book launch party. When my two sons and I arrived the day before, we couldn't find anybody at home or in the vineyard so we walked around town to kill time. An American flag flew from the tallest tower, it turned out, to honor the American publisher (though the mayor told me there had been an animated debate in the town council about it). A great party it was, with a walk to visit places mentioned in the book, speeches by the mayor, ex-mayor, the son and me, reminiscences from the audience, local wine for all, book signing, a banquet.

I told the story to the boss. A broad smile lightened his face.

GAS SHORTAGE

I don't like my job, he wrote to a friend. The commute, forty-one miles each way, is wearing me down.

And there is another gas shortage. The price is up, though still less than what you are paying. What hurts is the scarcity. I have to refuel twice a week but only a few stations are open and the lines are long. People are going crazy, and this is only the beginning. They are acting like I thought they would when the oil ran out, but I didn't think they would act this way so soon. It has only been two weeks.

Someone always tries to cut into line ahead of the rest. I've heard about fistfights. The other day someone cut into line just in front of me, so I beeped my horn and was ignored. I got out and walked up and told him the end of the line was back there. And he said now let's be human beings, human beings, human beings, I can't go back there because there's a double yellow line. I pointed out that everyone else had had the same problem, but he kept admonishing me to be a human being and we were all suffering so would I act like a human being. I tried to tell him he would have to suffer like the rest of us human beings and not cut into the line but he wouldn't listen and he wouldn't move so I tried to break off his rear view mirror. I think he was insane.

But what was I? Well, hell, I acted like a human being—I tried to do him harm.

My officemate reports that on the news last night was the story of a man who did what I did, but when he went up to the car he was stabbed to death. My officemate says that when people are brought up having everything they want and enter a situation where they can't have something, they go mad. And moreover the knife-wielder and the other guy lived in two different worlds, the former in a part of town where when someone walks up to your car he's going to injure you so you injure him first.

Lately I've been thinking that the animal in our nature, the uncontrolled greed and sadism, is not far beneath the surface. Decent people express horror when Idi Amin murders thousands and decent people say thank god we live here and that doesn't happen here and won't and couldn't and it probably hasn't actually happened anywhere else except long ago during World War Two. But I think these decent people have their heads up their asses. What Hitler and the Germans did is not ancient history. Some of them are still alive, and there are people like them everywhere.

But here we have only two weeks of long lines at gas stations, not food stations or clothing or shelter stations, not the Watts riots or the 68 Democratic convention or Appalachia or the Central Valley or general strikes, or even house heating oil, merely this comparatively insignificant irritant, we have two weeks of it and already murders. Even I am off my kilter.

The automobile is a terror. People feel they have no control over things, which indeed they do not. I think that in his car each man feels that there he is control. It's one of the few places a man's volition has effect. Another is the volume of his stereo or television. People feel they have a right to loud noise and 75 mph. Maybe they do. But surely other people have a right to quiet and to drive on the freeway without being threatened by maniacs insisting on their own rights. Before we moved from our old apartment we had a neighbor who told me I had to realize that in apartment living everyone has to put up with a certain intrusion into his privacy. He told me this when I asked him to turn down his stereo and TV a little. I was polite at first. I told him, yes, I agreed, and therefore he also had to put up with the intrusion into his privacy of keeping down his noise. The upshot was that he did keep the noise down somewhat but whenever he left he would crank it up tremendously loud for the last ten minutes.

My officemate also said that by the time these things happen in gas station lines, it's too late to do anything about it. Something should have been done when the people were children. It pains him when school funding, especially grade schools, is cut. He's a good man. But when I asked what we should do now, when these people are past grade school, he had no answer.

You can run from it. We moved from that apartment to one where things are better. Though there are problems here: The landlord is a speculator who doesn't want to maintain the building (though he wants to appear as though he is), and one neighbor is irritating this way and another that, but it's a nice place and the drawbacks aren't serious.

And I can get a new job and say goodbye to the jerks here, though there are jerks at any job. I think, though, that I may prefer the jerks in private industry to those in the government with their secure jobs and their years to retirement and their unlimited budgets. If I got one in the city I would at least avoid the commute and the gas lines. Though the ugly side of people on the freeway would not go away, I wouldn't see it and could look at a better side of things. Maybe by so doing I will join the decent people and forget man's inhumanity.

If things get worse, I can move away entirely. But where? A small town? The wilderness? The Far East?

No! Stand and Fight!

Hell, yes.

Fight whom? With what? With knives? Lawsuits? I am suing my old landlord for recovery of my cleaning deposit. Does this advance the cause of universal justice? Our agency is indeed limited.

Fight whom? Fight people for being thoughtless and un-kind? Not much you can do there. There's no forum for it, and if you confront them directly you only exasperate them and exacerbate your anxiety.

POTHOLES

I like to think of potholes as our little contribution to the war effort. The money we could have spent filling them is going to support our boys over in Afghanistan, and Iraq, and Czech Republic, Nigeria, Colombia, Indonesia, Uzbekistan, Syria, and all those other places where the War With No End In Our Lifetime Against Terrorism is being waged. Our streets might be a little bumpy, but they're safe, by god, thanks to our brave men and women and contractors. And though I myself can't lay down my life for my country, being a little long in the tooth and also a little too engaged in other activities, like President W was during Vietnam, I'm proud to offer the upkeep of our streets. And I don't mind if Halliburton and Blackwater and Lockheed Martin directors and shareholders make a few bucks instead of the local paving contractors. The money's got to go someplace, right?

As I've said elsewhere, I'm glad I don't live in the times of the Vandals and the Horde, but as I also said, at least in those days people called a spade a spade. Though I doubt that the spaded ones—the pillaged and the raped—took much consolation in knowing what to call it. These days, in this democratic system of ours, the bosses have to get the victims to consent to being pillaged. Or at least not object too loudly, though lately they seem to care less who squawks or how much.

How do they do it? Well for one thing, they don't call things by their names. The war for hegemony, for instance, is called The War on Terror. Cutting school funding is called No Child Left Behind. The privatization of the national retirement system is called Social Security reform.

For another thing, the pillage isn't direct. Bureaucracy

and the Federal Reserve Bank have replaced the Mongols' horses. Not a bad thing—the application of rules and regulations is surely better than brute force—but it's also a good cover for theft.

And for another, the rape isn't physical, except in places like Iraq and Afghanistan, and over there that's a war going on, after all, and anyway you know boys will be boys.

I don't think most people are fooled when Fox News reports that ExxonMobil's profit margin last year was lower than your corner grocery's. But people must not be seeing beyond their initial skepticism. They can't be putting the pieces together. Do they see the pieces? Do they even imagine there's a picture to be seen? What happened to critical thinking in America? They're surely not asking questions. Look—I'm an American who grew up here; I can't help comparing us to the Europeans I know, the Iranians, the Arab Middle-easterners—they ask questions. At least, they ask each other; in some places, granted, you shut up so you don't get arrested. Here in America nobody asks.

(Though I do know a couple Americans who asked too often, or the wrong things, and ended up in jail here—my son, my daughter, my ex-wife, my dad. Okay, they did more than ask: They asked while standing with some other people on a sidewalk, or in a parking lot, or walking across a bridge. They thought there was something in the Constitution that gave them the right to assemble and the freedom to ask. Well, there is. But that part isn't operative everywhere nowadays.)

You ask questions when you don't understand something. One reason you may not understand is that something is being obfuscated. In that case, a question may make people notice that the truth isn't being spoken, that there is dissimulation, lack of frankness, outright lie. The bosses don't like questions and suppress them one way or another.

But generally, nobody asks. Why? Here's a probably over-simplified suggestion: Americans believe in individualism and capitalism, and that each person can develop his talents, be the best she can be, be what he wants to be, or, to boil it down to what really counts, get rich. Every two-bit Cadillac dealer in Middle America thinks he can get the franchise for the whole state and get rich—if the god damned regulators would get off the businessman's back and give him a fighting chance. So to preserve his chance he votes against his day-to-day well-being. Give me riches or give me death!—or maybe, give me crappy schools but give me a shot at the lottery.

As for people capable of thinking past their own noses, the intellectuals in this country lead whatever debate there is along a narrow path. Questions are reasonable only if they remain within well-defined—though not necessarily overtly stated—bounds, and only reasonable questions are allowed. But this is well known. Edward S Herman and Noam Chomsky wrote a good book about it, *Manufacturing Consent*. We all know this.

This being an election year, the manufacturers are spinning away. Have you noticed? Have you noticed the false choices being offered? Democrat/Republican. Continued presence/endless war. Obama/McCain. Flip a coin—whichever side comes up, it's the same coin. What about stuff that's off the coin? Why aren't the media, even the so-called progressive media, reporting on Cynthia McKinney, Dennis Kucinich, Ron Paul, Lyndon LaRouche, Ralph Nader? I only ask.

Actually maybe Americans do vote more for their real interests than it appears. Maybe they are mean-spirited and selfish when it comes to helping themselves. Maybe they don't care that the outcome of the last couple of presidential elections wasn't what most voters had voted for. But I don't think so. We all know there's no reason for concern since it couldn't have happened here, where elections are free and fair, and sons don't inherit their fathers' offices.

Sorry, everybody. I don't mean to run down my favorite country, the place of my birth and tabernacle of my heart. Sometimes fantasy carries me off when I irresponsibly skip my meds. Or maybe it's my subversive wife. I don't know.

I just want to say that I'm proud to drive over potholes and thank you for joining me.

TURN SIGNALS

We moved to Marin County a couple years ago for its weather, beauty, and neighborliness, all of which we've very much enjoyed. One thing has puzzled us, though: How seldom people use their turn signals.

At first we thought we had joined a community of scofflaws, or perhaps that this was a mild manifestation of the renowned Marin spirit of creative independence, or that drivers concealed their intentions so as not to be forestalled before acting on them, or even that they didn't know they were going to turn until they had done it.

Then it occurred to us to pity a design flaw in all these expensive cars. Surely the turn signals were prone to early failure and drivers were simply conserving them for the time there was a real need to signal, and we gave some small thanks for our own car's lights which have operated trouble-free for years. That seemed unlikely, though, given that so many makes could not all have the same problem.

We think we have finally understood. The people of Marin, the longtime natives, that is, are so attuned to each other that they know when and which direction someone is going to turn. There is no need to signal—signaling is redundant. Alas, we despair of ever entering into this neighborly communality, but must say that it makes us appreciate all the more the tolerance with which we are accepted despite our psychic inadequacy.

Why Californians Won't Meet Your Eye

Imagine walking pleasantly along a sidewalk smiling at people you pass. Do you get more than a quickly averted glance in response, if that? Or imagine the tense silence in an elevator.

I used to think the French wouldn't meet your eye. They were devilishly unfriendly to strangers, although if you were introduced they were great, and to tell the truth, if you stopped someone to ask for directions he would usually give you an unhurried answer. Americans used to do that, and would sometimes accompany you halfway there to be sure you didn't get lost.

I'm generalizing, or course—I mostly meet only Californians. That is to say, the people I meet are in California because that's where I live, so I assume most of them are Californians. And because the places I go are cities and freeway rest stops and major parks, they're probably mostly urban.

I said hello to two men who came into the communal wash and toilet room at a campground in Mt Lassen National Park. Neither responded, neither returned my greeting, neither as much as grunted. The next morning I said hello to another man and later to a boy. No response. Maybe the boy was afraid that if he responded I would inflict some unspecified obscenity upon him. I understand. I am sensitive to women's concern about such things though I was surprised at the boy. I suppose he has been taught to stay away from strangers.

This behavior is more and more common. It is based mostly on fear, I think.

First, people are afraid you may ask them for something. Money, a favor, information; regardless of what you want, you'll be taking their time.

Next, they're afraid to get involved. Their feelings, their emotional energy, their commitment may be called upon. Their compassion is fatigued. Their capacity for interaction is depleted.

Three. Lack of savoir faire. They're not sure how to act with strangers. No customs have replaced the ones that were discarded when commercialism and advertising replaced interpersonal communication.

Four. Personal freedom, everyone's highest good, the freedom to do anything you want, to buy anything you want, includes the freedom, indeed the obligation, to dispense with courtesy, which is a constraint imposed upon you by others.

Five. Insecurity. They don't want to be found out to not know what they're supposed to know. They're being tested all the time. They might make a mistake. They might be found to be nonconformist.

Six. Arrogance. Especially the ones in their twenties and thirties. They're learning their roles in maintaining hegemony over the poorer classes and the rest of the world. If you're not with them, you're *infra*.

Seven. Hostility. A few are simply mean people who wouldn't give a cockroach the time of day.

THINGS NOT TALKED ABOUT

You have a liberation army marching through Iraq, say, or Haiti, or Panama, one of those places where the humanitarians in Washington, having realized the people are suffering too much under a dictator's boot, sent in the troops, US or coalition if they could gin up a coalition, and the conquering and victorious army is heading rapidly toward the capital when damned if—it happens every time—instead of entering the capital and taking out or at least capturing the evil dictator, and this, by the way, after killing hundreds, maybe thousands of soldiers and collaterals along the way, poor saps who were in the dictator's army to avoid starvation probably, and civilian saps who couldn't get out of the way or didn't want to leave their houses and possessions unattended while an invading army came through—and after losing a few of our own poor saps who joined in order to get out of the barrio or the ghetto—poor saps all—the unstoppable troops stop somewhere outside the city and the dictator escapes to a neighboring country and later resides in Monte Carlo or Johannesburg or Miami.

There seems to be an understanding among leaders everywhere to go only so far and then stop, a mutual aid society, mutual assistance pact, a kind of Big Shot Treaty Organization that says it's okay to kill and maim as many as you like below the rank of senator or brigadier general, say, but heads of state—kings, presidents, emperors, colonels—are granted professional courtesy. Immunity for the bosses.

(Though the current crop of bosses may be reneging on the deal. They kept Saddam Hussein and Slobodan Milosevic for show trials and actually executed them, and now they're

186

talking about impeaching Pervez Musharraf. Well, you do what you gotta do. If the SOBs won't leave when it's time to leave, they deserve what they get.)

Now, that's just a joke. Of course there is no such agreement.

But something else strange is going on.

We all know there's a consensus among leaders and the media to not talk about certain things: labor movements, anti-war and anti-nuclear power demonstrations, the privatization of natural resources and local utilities, and resistance thereunto. Bosses everywhere are for privatization and against popular movements, and media everywhere either belong to the bosses or operate at their sufferance, so it's not surprising they don't cover these subjects. Media don't cover what the bosses want kept quiet. This is so well known that to learn what the ruling class fears and suppresses, you only have to notice what isn't broadcast.

Have you noticed that the media don't talk about torture?

You wouldn't be surprised if a nation's media didn't talk about torture by its own people or its allies, but even when it's done by their so-called enemies? When broadcasting the facts would make good propaganda?

Now, this particular ban isn't always and everywhere true. For example, Alexander Solzhenitsyn was published. But did you notice that he was also subtly discredited in the Western press? You would expect the Soviets to run him down, but the US media basically made him out to be an intransigent moralist, a weirdo fundamentalist Christian fanatic. (How could you not be an intransigent moralist, knowing what he knew?) And there was some coverage of Abu Ghraib, and now and then a bit of tut-tutting about My Lai, and from time to time some finger-wagging about Fallujah or Guantanamo.

And something about waterboarding. What was that all about, for Christ's sake? Isn't it a cross between surfing and skateboarding? Look, I'm sure being forced to skateboard in the hot sun ain't exactly your idea of a good time. But torture? Jon Stewart, I think it was, made a good point when he said something like: Abu Ghraib doesn't matter—what matters is that we're not the kind of people who torture other people.

Me too, by the way, I'm proud to be an American who doesn't torture other people.

Apart from that, may I point out the unusual recent post by the Association of Iranian Political Prisoners called "Blind-folded Witnesses." Such a sober description and frank discussion of torture is seldom produced and rarely available to a mass audience. Its makers merely report like Solzhenitsyn what happened, when, who did it, what it felt like; and their plain candor and lack of rhetoric is heart-breaking.

There were some other posts in 2006 that describe torture in Iran in 1986 and 1987. According to the author, these articles were written soon afterwards and were offered at the time to major magazines in the West, and they were read by major academic figures in the US, but no one was interested in publishing this significant news.

This is a curious thing. Remember that US foreign policy then was as virulently anti-Iran as it is now. Wouldn't you think that articles about torture and execution in Iranian prisons would have made good propaganda? Why weren't they picked up? It wasn't for lack of the right people seeing them. Was it that the author was unknown? Hell, articles by imaginary authors containing fabricated information are published all the time, especially before, during, and after wars. What could it have been but the subject matter?

Okay, so torture is one of those topics that aren't covered. Why? That is today's question.

Is it because they all do it? All the bosses use torture? And they know they're sinners and don't want to cast the first stone? They actually are the Christians they say they are? (We're talking about the US leaders, now.) They have compassion for their sinful enemies? Or could it be that they don't want to accuse others lest they be accused themselves? They don't want to ignite a spotlight that might be swung round to shine upon themselves?

Do the bosses keep this quiet so they don't demoralize

their own people? Would their people feel bad if they knew their neighbors and cousins and sons and daughters were torturing somebody else's neighbors and cousins and sons and daughters? Wouldn't their people be upset? Are the bosses keeping up morale at home by keeping the pictures pretty and Disneyfied?

The leaders themselves don't apply the pliers, but don't they convey with winks and nods and memoranda that it should be done? Does anyone resist orders from the boss? Can they? If they're in the army, what's the choice? Do torturers do it against their better judgment? Do they have judgment, these twenty-year-old uneducated kids from trailer parks? If they do, how easily is it overwhelmed by direct command and peer pressure?

Or do torturers do it willingly? Are they ordinary people or does a certain vicious personality gravitate toward this kind of work? How fast can an army sort itself into such specialists? Do powerless people enjoy asserting themselves, exercising control, being boss for a day? Do they enjoy hurting other people? Do kids like pulling wings off flies? Do people take their lead from their leaders? If the guy in charge condones cruelty, does everyone become more cruel? Is cruelty so easy to invoke that it only takes a couple years of a leader's term in office?

Is torture always approved by the guy in charge? Would anybody below the guy in charge approve torture on his own? Would you yourself give someone the order to torture? Would you torture if you were given the order?

Are the bosses ashamed of what they do? Why would they be ashamed of torture, when they're not ashamed of everything else they do in pursuit of riches and power?

And what do you do with the torturers when the regime changes?

Just wondering.

THE DEATH OF THE PAST

"Among the broad scatters of broken pottery and wind-eroded mounds that mark the remains of the world's first cities in the desolate landscape of Southern Iraq, ancient mud structures, never recovered as much more than ground plans, disintegrate soon after they are excavated." (Paul Zimansky Times Literary Supplement, 7 August 2015.)

We are mining our past as we are extracting the fuels of fossils 300 million years old. When the fuels are gone, what will we do? When our history has been exposed and as a result deteriorates, what history will be left for our descendants in 2,000 years? Is everything for us? Do we care? Will there be descendants in 2,000 years?

We have found fossils, shards, scrolls, sites, ruins; we have carefully gathered, understood and tried to preserve them; we have amassed more knowledge of the past than ever was—but the knowledge is stored in our notoriously forgetful minds and in media whose longevity is questionable. The knowledge is no longer sheltered by the earth. Will things last as long again as they already have? Have we mined our past as we have greedily extracted other natural resources? What will happen when it's all been used?

Maybe it doesn't matter. If our species dies along with the millions of other species it has exterminated in its blind development of creature comfort, then it may as well enjoy its past however fleeting. What matter that excavated items deteriorate within a century if the species who found them no longer exists?

Herculaneum and Pompeii are coming to light. "Workers have painstakingly restored several two-story stone houses, piecing together original lintels of wood carbonized by the explosion—sealed for 2,000 years in their oxygen-less tomb..." (Smithsonian Magazine, July-August 2015.) But now that the lintels are exposed to oxygen, how long will they last?

RETRO

The past is mined and recycled to the point of ennui, and the Smithsonian Institution and National Geographic Society are not the only extractionists.

Pop culture eats and regurgitates its own past. It lives on recombinations. Bands cover earlier songs; DJs put fragments of them into new music; TV documentaries extend only back to the beginning of filmed images. Modernism was a great recycler; TS Eliot was a great collagist making new poetry out of old. Creativity is now the careful juxtaposition of images and thoughts that already exist.

We are obsessed with the artifacts of our own immediate past. We are obsessed with our present—think soup cans.

Artists who have to make a living know that if something was successful, its repetition should also be successful. Consumers like the familiar and not the new, which requires concentration and thought by all. Luckily for artists, combinations of the same material are inexhaustible.

NOSTALGIA

Wretched is he whose heart is not here, who yearns for the past, who pines for a world far away.

I.   All thoughts center on the place left behind.

II.   In particular, they center on good aspects of the place. No one is nostalgic for bad things.

III.   The yearning cannot be assuaged because its cause is loss, which can be soothed only by restoring what was lost, by bringing the past here, to now; but we cannot do that—we can only remember, and memory is only an image.

IV.   However, memory is necessary for nostalgia. Without memory there is no connection to the past, no continuity, no history, and we repeat ourselves unconscious of our repetition, like dogs (who do not suffer from nostalgia). But forgetting to observe ourselves remembering, or over-emphasizing a recollection, or even single-minded concentration—imbalance, that is—prevents assimilation, contentment, happiness.

We seek comfort in a strange place by recalling the familiar past.

Or because we are not happy we think back to better times, to the good life then.

Present difficulties and ennuis are forgotten, but the comfort is disturbed and incomplete since it is shot with regret for what is gone.

Events from then or there are rehashed with friends as if

they were current affairs. But we are powerless to affect them, nor can we but barely affect events here and so our universal lack of agency is another cause for regret.

The place left behind occludes the place we occupy. As in wan moonlight we pick through a colorless landscape by recalling it in daylight, so thoughts and emotions are referred to that other sparkling place. What happens here means naught. If only this were happening there—then it would count for something.

A cultured and accomplished Iranian lady who was forced to leave by the 1979 revolution:
"Tamerlane was a Turk who viciously slaughtered the Persians. He conquered everyone from Anatolia to China. Then he was so impressed by the Persian culture that he built schools, patronized calligraphy, and practiced religious toleration.
"He called himself 'son-in-law' because he married a descendant of Genghis Khan. Genghis Khan destroyed what he did not understand, but not Tamerlane. He had a painting made. At the top it said 'son-in-law' and at bottom were lines from the Koran, showing that he placed himself higher than Islam.
"The miniatures produced under his reign and his sons' were a combination of Persian and Turkish, not as good as pure Persian, in my opinion, which is somehow finer, not as coarse as Turkish."
And the Persians also invented baseball. Or was it the Russians? And who invented the spaghetti Marco Polo brought back? Ask a homesick emigrant.

V.   Nostalgie de la boue is a craving to degrade ourselves while maintaining our social status. Not at all the same thing.

THE KORAN

It's the same god as the Jewish and the Christian, nothing new here.

Repetitious

The stories of Moses, Abraham, Noah, Ad, Thamood,
Lot, Shuaib, Iblis, etc, are told over and over again. There
are few stories, and they are mostly Old Testament.

Basic tenets

Believe.
Pray.
Give alms.

The main theme is belief vs nonbelief

Unbelievers will be chastised.
Unbelievers may live affluent, privileged lives, but god may
destroy them, and they will assuredly go to hell when they die.
God predetermines whether one will believe or not. (If so,
how can an unbeliever be converted? Not explained.)
The worst evil is disbelief after having been given the
signs of God.
Believe! If you do, heaven; if not, hell.
On one occasion, God did not chastise some unbelievers
because there were believers among them.
Don't consort with unbelievers.

Why believe in God?

Because the prophets tell us to.
Because God created the world.

Commands

There is no God but God.
Honor thy father and mother.
Respect contracts (bear not false witness).
Commit not adultery, scourge is 100 stripes – Hammurabi.
Respect the property of orphans (steal not, special case).
Beat your wife if you suspect her of... [one thing or another].
Very anti-usury and pro-alms.

Proofs of the existence of God

Day and night exist.
He created us.
We are mortals.
He created spouses for us.
He created the heavens and earth.
He created the variety of tongues and hues.
We sleep at night.
He makes it rain.
Heaven and earth stand firm on his command.
The ships run on the seas.
No one else is capable of creation.

Good things

Surrender, belief, obedience, truth, endurance, humility, charity, fasting, chastity, prayer.

Bad things

Cowardice in battle, usury.

Jack Oakley

Miscellaneous

Prophets have often been disbelieved, on the grounds that they are mortal. There is much concern to establish the Messenger Mohammad's authority.

God created men to be returned to him (not for mere sport).

It is okay for the Prophet but not believers to take female cousins as wives.

God knows all.

"Be as my mother's back." ??

TUMBLING WORDS

The words that tumble from your gaunt and bearded and so sympathetic face, as you pour hot water into my cup of instant coffee in the yellow morning light found only in this place, calmly, thoroughly explicate something I barely start to grasp because my French is not as good as I have always pretended and you've consequently assumed that I've understood. Stupid me. Instead of nodding and throwing in a word appropriate to some small phrase I've grasped, I should have risked your patience and asked for repetition or translation each time I failed to catch your meaning. I have a six-year-old and know how trying it is to repeat and explain everything—even when you do it for your dearest ones—but I have ended up understanding very little because I've feared my interruptions would lessen the pleasure you take in rambling on to an attentive listener.

You are one of the people dearest to me. Because of your demeanor, surely, since I don't know what you're saying—it's the way you say it! Well, I'm not quite so simple. I do follow your sense of humor, your sense of right and wrong and the absurd, your outrage at the cruelty of the powers that be, your concern for my happiness.

Three Good Boys and a Couple of Bad Ones

I was relaxing on our cabin porch at San Francisco's family camp in the Sierras, a great place to spend a week, where the kids get on their bikes at breakfast, check in a couple times during the day, and otherwise ride until bedtime from the lake to the swimming pool, dining hall, and each other's cabins. This evening my eight-year-old son was at the outdoor stage with some other kids practicing for the talent show later on. Three boys rode up—eleven or twelve years old, I'd guess. The oldest asked if I was the dad of a kid with a shiny blue helmet. If I was, he said, he had sort of bad news.

I am, I said, tell me, hoping that Lex wasn't at the nurse's cabin after crashing into a tree.

It's kind of bad news, he said. I don't know if it's right to tell you.

Please do, I said. I sat up to show that I would take him seriously.

He and his friends explained that they had been on the stage rehearsing their skit when they grew aware of a younger girl and boy sitting in the benches making noise and heckling. My son told the troublemakers to be quiet and then grabbed the boy by the hair. The boy started squealing. His father arrived just then and yelled at Lex for a while and then left with his son. The boys said they didn't want me to be upset but thought I should know about it because the man had been so angry.

Lex rode up and said he'd ridden by two or three times but had been afraid to stop in case I was mad.

One of the boys told him, no, you shouldn't be afraid, you should always tell your parents what happened. Another added that your parents never get mad if you tell them what happened. Believe us, we know, said the third, it's happened to us many times.

Lex sat on the picnic table bench looking shrunken and lonely. I sat next to him and put my arm around him and asked what happened.

Don't be afraid to do the things you want to do, said the oldest, don't be afraid of the guy. Yeah, said the others, don't let him bully you. You have a right to be here too. If we can give you some advice, they said, from now until the end of the week don't touch anybody or even yell at anybody, because now that this happened, it'd look really bad. If you don't do anything else, you'll be okay.

Let's go apologize, I said. That's the best thing to do.

I walked and they rode. Don't ride too fast, I said, or I won't be able to keep up. The boys slowed their pace to mine. They took me to the stage and pointed to the nearest cabin. That's it, they said. We're going to go back to the stage. Thank you, I said, I really appreciate what you've done, taking the trouble to come and tell me.

As Lex and I approached the cabin the father was walking up the path. I had seen him and his son at the lake a couple days earlier in an inflatable canoe near the raft where the kids hung out. The boy wore a lifejacket and his father a wetsuit with a hood, which struck me as slightly bizarre given how warm it was. He put on a mask and snorkel and dove into the water. Given how murky it was, I couldn't imagine what he could possibly see. He struck me as the kind of crackpot who damns the torpedos and bullheads straight ahead despite public opinion, the kind of dad a kid would be mortified to have, as I had told my wife. A day later, though, I heard the boy bragging that his father had found a necklace. I thought the boy had learned how to make the best of things.

Now I saw that he was a fairly big man, and he shaved his head and wore an earring.

I'm Jack, I said, and this is Lex.

I'm Jimmy, he said.

I could see that he wanted to do the talking, so I let him. I didn't have much to say anyway. We had come to deliver a simple apology.

He talked. It did him good to get it off his chest.

I said we'd come to apologize.

Lex said, I'm very, very sorry.

The man said thank you, let's go find Clayton so you can apologize to him.

The next day I saw Clayton at the dance by the general store. He was in a fencer's pose, threatening another child with a light stick that he held like a sword. His mother calmly asked him to stop. It looked like she was accustomed to asking him to stop.

The father avoided meeting my eye the next couple days.

The day after our return home, we bumped into a classmate of Lex's with his father at the park. It turned out that his neighbors had also just returned from the camp. It turned out that his neighbors were these people.

The mother works and the father stays home taking care of the kids, Lex's friend's father said. He didn't think much of his neighbor. He was rough on the boys, a disciplinarian, and something of an oddball. The older boy was well-behaved but the younger was a troublemaker.

Well, so was mine sometimes, when frustration overcame his affability, but we must overcome our frustration or it gets us into all kinds of trouble.

I'd been very impressed that the boys had known who was staying where in the 120 cabins and 20 tents, and this after only five days. Smart, observant boys.

DUCK HUNTING ON THE MISSISSIPPI

My Grampa was a member of a duck hunting club that kept a couple blinds and a cabin on Sourwine Island. When my dad was a boy they raised mallards at home that they took to the river during hunting season. Lines called stagings ran from pens on the shore to a weight several yards out in the water. They were like trotlines but shorter. A ring around the staging was attached to a line called a snood with a clip at the other end that was attached to a ring around a duck's leg. Thus tethered, the duck swam around as a decoy.

Other ones named call ducks or Judas ducks were kept in the blind until a wild group flew over. The call ducks were trained to fly up, join the wild ones, and talk them into coming down.

"What did they say to bring the wild ones down?"

"I don't know. I don't speak duck. Well, a little, but I don't know the whole language."

"How did you keep from shooting the call ducks?"

"Oh, they would swim in to shore. Then we'd stand up and shoot the wild ones."

Sometimes the wild ducks would be a mile high and keep right on going. They wouldn't come down for anything. The best time was evenings or mornings when they were ready for a rest.

Across the dirt lane from my Grampa's place at the river lived some poor white trash in shacks that trespassed on somebody's shorefront. They lived by fishing.

"We left them alone but once some men from the club chopped up nets they found in a lake at the south end of the island. 'That'll teach them to put nets in the lake!' they said."

The cabin burned down the following winter. "It was two stories with a screened porch around two sides. We have a picture of it somewhere. We replaced it with a cabin of hewn logs with small windows on three sides. It was very basic— just someplace to get out of the weather. We had gas lamps and a gas stove."

Trotlines were fishing lines that ran from the bank into the water. You pulled them in and checked the hooks every couple days. When people started dragging the bottom for clams, they tore up a lot of trotlines, so the fishermen started laying jump lines out in the river in the evening and returning the next morning to haul them in. One end had a float, an empty plastic bottle, so you could find it, and the other end a weight.

Jump lines had a hundred snoods with hooks. The jumpline was coiled in a shallow box with quarter-inch mesh on the bottom and twenty-five notches in each side where the hooks dangled on the outside. "You baited them with Catalpa worms when they were in season or worms or chopped up fish.

"You drove the boat slow and dropped the weight in and made sure nothing got tangled as the line ran into the water, turning the box after each side was out. Then you stopped and tied the float to the end. If you dropped the line before the float was on, it was a devil of a time dragging for it on the bottom and most often you lost it. Most everybody knew enough to tie the float on before they threw the weight in.

"In the morning it was fun to feel the fish as you pulled the line in. What was it going to be?"

They took catfish, perch and gar, though the perch were too bony to eat and the gars didn't taste good. You'd club the gar on the head with a piece of pipe to kill it and throw it back because they ate other fish.

My dad still owns 1/40 of 137 acres on Sourwine Island (spelled Sauerwine in 1930; everybody around there pronounces it "Sarrawine"), Big Willow Bar, and Little Willow Bar, 128 acres on Burlington Island, and 3.4 acres on Big Island, unless one of the bars has washed away. He's in touch with the other owners that he could find, thinking to sell his share so his kids won't have to deal with it when he dies.

CONSERVATION

Mr C works to conserve a portion of bay wetlands for wild-life and some for a park, an educational park with wooden paths and explanatory signs and probably also a picnic area and maybe a beach. He'd rather keep it all for wildlife but will need supporters so he sets aside land for people. Political compromise.

How much for people? 50/50? The less the better. But try figuring it out rationally—it'll be easier to sell. Divvy it up by body mass. People and animals. Small animals get small spaces. How much does an individual need? Individual of a given species. There's not a lot of information so he makes some wild guesses for starters. Can change later.

What species are living there now? He estimates the number around the bay. He estimates the number of individuals. Bugs, migratory birds, plants. Of course plants, he'd overlooked them, being faunocentric.

How much space per body, square centimeter per gram? The amount of available space is undetermined. He has to propose the figure. Start with an arbitrary area, divide by space needed for a species, determine the number of species that can live there. Microscopic organisms need microscopic space so he ignores them. They can fit in the cracks. But some species need other ones to survive, too. How to know which?

A given area will support a certain number of species. Is there a point below which the whole thing won't make sense? Too few species and a viable community is impossible. How many? Which ones?

How much area for people? Pick a number. How many species will the remaining area support? Do people really need that much? Do they want that much? How much per person? How many people at a time? Too few people and a viable campaign is impossible. Should there be a gift shop? Snack stand? Take a poll. Can't. No money. Need backers. Pick a smaller number. Now how many species?

Lots of moving pieces. He develops a spread sheet, a database, micros and macros to track them. Finds that his personal computer can't keep up. Scavenges a server, another; fills them with variables and data. Calls a friend at Scripps who is interested and finds time for him on their climate-modeling supercomputer. Others get interested and soon a grad student is working on it.

The calculations grow, an article is published in Science, the marshes are drained and developed and Mr C barely notices.

MASTER BUFON

(Homage to Roberto Bolaño)

Bufon (973–1059) Japanese

> *...all this, however, was ultimately discarded.*

> *After his early struggles to refine the expression of these ideas, Bufon "laid aside his scribbling" for some fourteen years as he reassessed his positions. In 1017 he recorded his first attempt at a synthesis of the four fundamental concepts and in late fall penned the charac- ter for "rock," whose bleak view of the ultimate nature of things...*

Beginning students of poetry sometimes wonder why collections of haiku include only a single work consisting of a single word by a poet known as Master Bufon, and their perplexity increases upon learning that this is his only poem.

1. Why is this short piece considered a masterpiece?
2. Compare and contrast *Rock* with *Paper* by Xenophenes.
3. For extra credit, discuss the character for scissors.

Time to Move On

Staying in one place is painful. Things seen again and again grow dull; their first fresh evocations have faded into the smooth ungranulated passage of days. It is time to find surroundings that are as they are themselves, without memories.

CHRONOS

As he languidly swung his scythe the world shuddered and fell with slowly growing speed to crash upon the beach where hungry waves lapped and ground it to pebbles and finally sand.

Seek and You Will Find, or Don't Seek

People walk together at the bottom of the layer of protein extending upward fifty meters, on the same plane of thoughts, responses, intellect, though we make a big deal out of the differences—the Cat and the Prot, the Hindu, Serb and Croat, poor man, rich man, villager and city folk and so on—but similar enough for government work. I could walk up to that scruffy-looking deliveryman and ask directions to somewhere and he would tell me. He shows up for work, delivers things, cares about promotion, follows the White Sox. Maybe he beats his wife. How would I know?

The Buddhists feel compassion for all this protein. Not the stones and star clouds too? Oh yes. They do.

A woman walks by in a tight sweater that limns her well-shaped jouncing breasts. My eyes are drawn. Of the unceasing surrounding motion they select this one to follow. And now it fades into the background like everything else.

Suddenly the walking people and the newsstand, the street and buildings appear to be of the same cloth. Things are sharp and clear. My vision is perfect.

This must be satori. Me, here, unexpectedly.

Why me and why now?

What a pleasant treat.

Maybe it's the cigar and coffee. Maybe I'm having a heart attack. But what matter?

My Novel

The novel I wanted to write would have conveyed the vastness of time and space, generations of people, a story that began long ago and will continue after the last page, a sense of timelessness and eternity. From the intimate to the vast, the slow passage of minutes alongside the speedy transformations of epochs. Also the weirdness of existence.

About people, naturally, since stories are about people, but also about the landscapes and animals and plants we live with, and the immensity of galaxies and the coziness of burrows. The movement of people would show change on the scale we feel (the human), and the movement of continents and life's evolution would show it on another. I wanted to show man's connection to the world, his inextricable involvement with it, for he is of it. I thought this would be something new in literature, though I later learned that it would be new only in Western literature, or more precisely Western thought, and in fact only the most recent; but learning other ways of thinking would be some of the changes that I portrayed.

Overall the novel would give a sense of wholeness, a reassurance that things make sense, though it is we who make the sense where there is none; we create it, we bring it into being out of nothing—*fiat significatio*—we share it, and for a moment, reading the book, someone would feel comfort in the face of eeriness, would feel that there is sense in the world, albeit transitory and contingent, that there is sense in addition to everything else, and what a comfort to feel for a moment that someone else also felt it.

My book would have been like *War and Peace, A la recherche du temps perdu, The Brothers Karamazov, Les Thibaults, The Magic Mountain, Les Misérables, A Dance to the Music of Time.*

And This, I Think, Is My Life

I will miss my life when it's gone, though when I'm gone of course I will miss nothing. But the thought of its loss makes me mourn as I mourned my sister and mother and father.

I may have lived the most blessed life that a human could: childhood in an optimistic time when knowledge grew and my country's hegemony was total, comfort and travel and social tolerance increased, and there were immense flocks of birds and animals and abundant clean water. As I matured the last of the world was explored and explained and connected, and I passed through my own season of ripeness. Now as I age and lose vigor and breath and begin to ache, it grows apparent that the earth has been used up and spent, species go extinct by millions, the temperature rises and the tipping point has passed. I rue my children and theirs if there be any who survive. The world and I grew and declined together—lucky me—though so sad at my nearing death and the death of my loved ones and our race.

And when we're gone we will miss nothing. But the thought of our loss makes me mourn.

There is no hope, but we must live as if there were, not only for the vanishingly small chance of correcting our path in time to survive, but for our peace of mind.

At least these days I have learned to recognize beauty, and I shall enjoy as best as I can what remains of it all.

My testament: Beethoven's piano sonata op. 31, no. 2 for beauty, and the adagio from his piano sonata op. 106 for beauty and sorrow both, and Shostakovich's viola sonata op. 147 for anguish, and Beethoven's piano sonata op. 111 for his farewell to this rough magic.

www.ingramcontent.com/pod-product-compliance
Lightning Source LLC
Chambersburg PA
CBHW031416250626
47155CB00004B/1508